For Ever Again

Trevor Lockwood

*For Nancille
My lovely friend*

Trev

Braiswick

for

Jonathan and Kate

Braiswick
Felixstowe, Suffolk

ISBN 978-0-9557008-1-1
Copyright © 2007 Trevor Lockwood

All rights reserved. No part of this publication may be reproduced, stored in a retrieval system, or transmitted, in any form or by any means without the prior permission in writing of the publisher.

This book is sold subject to the condition that it shall not, by way of trade or otherwise, be lent, resold, hired out or otherwise circulated without the publisher's prior consent in any form other than that supplied by the publisher.

British Library Cataloguing in Publication Data available.

Cover design by Eileen Aldous

Printed by Lightning Source
Braiswick is an imprint of Catherine Aldous Design Ltd

Café Life

As she entered the restaurant Louise spotted him immediately. He was sitting at a table looking slightly uncomfortable in a jacket that had seen better days, a half-finished cup of coffee in front of him. She had the photo he had emailed the week before, and although it was a younger version that had stared almost coquettishly back at her from the computer screen it was without doubt the same man. He didn't look like a Harry, but then what does Harry look like?

She had given up smoking several weeks before and immediately regretted the decision, she may now run to fat. No real sign so far, but she did feel hungry. Hopefully he'd suggest lunch.

They talked, or rather he talked and she listened. Not that it wasn't interesting. It turned out that he was as fanatical about the business of writing and publishing as she was, but her attentions were compulsively drawn to the menu, it had been almost half an hour since she'd had a mid-morning snack. Now, she wondered, should she have a steak sandwich with French fries and salad, or go for the three-course meal, which involved a rather tempting chocolate mousse? For a while she hedged her bets as they opened their conversation. Finally, after much deliberation, they both decided to go for the business lunch, main course, with starter or dessert She was rather miffed at having to decide between the mousse and compote of wild mushrooms on puff pastry. But there was no competition really. She scraped her spoon around the bowl making sure she gathered up every conceivable remnant of chocolate, and sucked the spoon clean.

He coughed rather loudly.

"I said, are you from London originally or another migrant?"

"Oh, sorry, yes, I come from Surrey originally, Brindover. My parents still live there. I go home every so often."

"That's funny, I once belonged to a Lodge down there. Sorry, better get it out in the open as soon as possible but I've been a bit of a part-time freemason in the past."

"Are you, what a coincidence."

Her father was also a mason. He had regaled the family, rather unprofessionally, with tales of masonic deeds for the past ten years or so, including the baring of breasts, rolled up trouser legs and something to do with a goat, although that last may have been an old joke. The family had always hoped his loose tongue wouldn't cost lives.

It was the start of a wonderful, if rather tempestuous relationship.

* * *

She's not bad, thought Harry, as he peered over the top of the coffee cup. She has eyes that sparkle as she speaks and her lips invite a response. Her hair is clearly well-cut but not prissy; the sort that would look good all tangled up and framed by pillows. He liked her casual look, the soft blouse, blue jeans, not too much make-up, and very little jewellery. In fact, he smiled inside as he remembered the old joke, in fact, if she was lying naked in the gutter saying 'take me, take me', I'd find it hard to turn it down. This was a woman. A real woman.

He stood up, to adjust himself to the little black chair on which he was perched, suddenly conscious of his own body. He'd been sitting around too much, hunched over a computer and was now worried about his physique. He didn't really have a beer belly, not from where he was sitting anyway and now he no longer had a full-length mirror in his bedroom all was well. Summer was coming, a few less pints, a bit of exercise and he would shed a few pounds, all would be well. Perhaps she'd be able to help him lose a little weight? He tucked the cane chair under his bottom and tried once again to get comfortable. He smiled as he sat down. Vigorous exercise with her. That would be great.

"So have you sent your manuscript to any publishers yet?"

"No, I'm waiting until it's finished, it needs quite a bit of polishing, " she said, and then without pause, "what's it really about anyway?" She spoke softly as if she was pre-occupied in some way, not really concentrating.

Harry decided to ignore what she was saying and bluster on, she was probably just a little shy. After all it's not every day you physically meet somebody you have only known via the Internet. He talked about publishing, not that he really knew very much about the business although he had written one book but that was about the causes of crime. To be fair that book had not found a publisher and, on reflection, he rather wished it had never been written. He was now embarrassed to continue with the bravado he'd presented on his Blog and by email. He'd thought popular crime coming from the horse's mouth would attract publishers like bees round a honey pot. It was a disappointment to find out it wasn't like that.

Not that he told her anything of this. He plunged on throwing together odd snippets he had gained from magazines, conversations with friends, radio and television documentaries to form a gushing amalgam of stories. He didn't say these tales were about him just hoped that would be accepted. In turn, she nodded, smiled occasionally and flashed those eyes enough to keep up his momentum. As he talked his mind was racing. He was going to have this one. His eyes often lingering on the fluttering fall of satin over the gentle hillocks of her breasts as she breathed and moved.

She had decided that this mock French café with spindly chairs and barely filled plates was suitable for their first meeting. As it turned out he would have been pleased to take her into his local pub for a couple of pints and a plate of steak and kidney and the chance to bask in the admiring glances he knew would have come their way from the regulars. Maybe next time. He wanted there to be a next time. That was confirmed when she ran her spoon round the rim of her plate and slowly sucked off the last drop of her chocolate mousse..

Harry took another long look at the woman across the table. What did her mother look like? His mind played games for a few moments, seeing her as she matured. The shape of her back, the taking a slight droop to the chin, hair turning grey. He'd have to see her mother. After all daughters turn out to look just like their mothers. And behave the same way. That was a little trick he'd learnt from two disastrous marriages. Look at the mother-in-law. She can tell you everything about the woman beneath those lustful desires.

As they finished the meal, both lingering over coffee, he began to feel a sense of panic. Fine, They had both responded to emails, as professionals, each believing the other had some useful information to impart. Theirs was not a chat-line romance. They had not set out to find a partner, There was no, "See you on the corner duckie, I'm the one with the red carnation and enormous nob". This meeting had never been intended. It had just happened.

They discovered they lived close to each other. He had made the suggestion they should meet, partly because he had hoped to have gained some information that would be useful, but really it had just seemed like a bit of a laugh. A coincidence giving him an opportunity that could not be ignored. There had been a few jokey emails, with him finally pressing the need to meet for further discussion. Now they were together, what was there to discuss? It was now clear their writing had little in common. He was a copper. She? He wasn't sure what she was. A writer? Perhaps.

He rocked back on his chair, feeling the legs scrape across the tiled floor as he stamped both his feet firmly back on the ground to save himself from toppling over. The chubby waitress threw a chequered glance at him as she tottered past. Suddenly he felt very embarrassed. He leant forward, both arms sprawled across the marble-topped table; a coffee cup fell over spilling its meagre contents over the white surface.

"Can I." He hesitated, glancing away through the open doors into the street to where the lunchtime crowds were scurrying back and forth in an endless stream. He came back to her, looking directly into her eyes as he murmured, "Can I read some of your work?"

* * *

Read her book? Read her book! Louise thought as she marched up the road with him, and why had he insisted on walking with her? His legs looked shorter than hers, but his stride was obviously longer and she found herself almost running along behind him as he hurtled up the High Street in the direction of the department store, behind which her car was parked. When he had asked if he could read some of her work she had said yes, automatically, but a cold fear had gripped her stomach. An anonymous publisher, a bored agent, an even more bored reader, yes, but someone who she would have to look in the eye, or speak directly to on the phone, no. But it was too late she had committed herself.

To make matters worse she needed to pee, badly. His pace did not slacken and each movement of her legs reverberating up into her bladder was agony. She should have gone in the restaurant but she hadn't wanted to get up and walk away from the table knowing full well that his eyes would be firmly positioned on her bottom as she walked through the tables to the toilet door marked 'femme'.

Harry was a charmer there was no doubt about that. He had a way with women, which she knew was a dangerous element to contend with. She was prone to falling for men with a chat-up line, men who appeared to listen even if they weren't, men who revealed that they found her attractive by the way they looked at her, and often, on that basis alone, hadn't been able to refuse them. The fact that these men were usually indiscriminate in their affections and had a penchant for women of any size, shape or form, just as long as they had the requisite amount of equipment, and weren't too ugly, although that didn't always put them off, usually wasn't enough to put her off either.

That was all before Justin. She was with Justin now. Practically married. They were married enough not to see very much of each other. He was always off with his mates, playing rugby in the winter, cricket in the summer, squash and tennis. She was starting to think he was chasing his lost youth. It was getting a bit too much for an man in his forties to be chasing balls all the time.

He had mentioned a number of 'women' as they chatted at the table, in fact, he had confessed to two ex-wives and a number of hangers-on, although he didn't appear to be in a serious relationship with any of the latter. She didn't really want to become another notch on his headboard but for some peculiar glitch in her personality it made him seem all that more attractive. And besides she had an ex-husband and several eager hangers-on too and, although she hadn't felt inclined to mention it, a partner she was living with, Justin.

Louise looked at him out of the corner of her eye as they headed into the department store. He had that rumpled look about him, and although he was somewhat older than her, and was a bit overweight he carried himself well. There was a lot of dark brown hair, swept back off his forehead, reaching down to his collar, dark eyes, with a complexion that was smooth and tanned. In fact, he looked remarkably like a younger version of her father, which caused her to stumble slightly as they approached the back entrance of the store.

"Careful, there." He grabbed her arm with one hand and placed the other on her waist. She felt a small shiver of anticipation ripple through her.

"It's these shoes, silly things, I shouldn't have bought them, they keep slipping off my feet."

"Fashion victim?"

"Yes, look," she said, pushing the double doors open, "you don't have to walk all the way with me."

"I'll see you to your car."

"I was going to do some shopping on the way home so I might say goodbye now."

"Oh, okay then... sorry... I just thought... no never mind... it's been really nice, we must do it again."

"Yes, I enjoyed it to."

"Which floor?"

She hesitated before replying, he wasn't going to leave her that easily.

"Five."

He followed her up the steps and she knew he had got his chance and flexed her buttocks together, which sent an agony of movement through her bladder.

"Here we are." She fumbled in her handbag for the keys.

"Its been wonderful." He stood in front of her. "I've really enjoyed it; in fact I haven't enjoyed myself so much for a long time."

"It has, me too." She found her keys, and fumbled for the lock. She wanted to put a barrier between them, and the car door was as good as any.

She jumped into the seat and wound the window down.

"Right."

He leaned into the open window. Their heads clashed as she turned a cheek towards his puckered lips and he moved to kiss her full on the mouth.

"Sorry." They both jerked heads out of harm's way.

"Look, call me." He said, his eyes fixed intently on her face.

"Yes, I will. Anyway, I've got to email some of my work to you."

"No, I mean call me, really. I…"

"Yes, I will, I promise."

Harry watched her drive away, a sporty green car, small but sleek. She was? She was intriguing and seemed amenable yet somehow he felt chastened. That was the end of that then. He'd made his desperation seem so obvious, what on earth had possessed him. Shame, he thought, thinking of that bottom in those jeans as she slipped into her car. He'd been around women a long time, made enough mistakes to know when he'd made another. It was tempting to say it was nothing to do with him. She'd said she had a meeting that afternoon, had to rush away. That left him cold because she'd also said she wanted to do some shopping. Once he'd made a decision there was a job to be done. So far that didn't seem to be moving quite the way he wanted. Never mind. He'd let it mature awhile, there was plenty of time. She was one to savour, not to be rushed.

Back home he sent her an email; 'Good to put a face to your words thanks for a lovely day. We should do it again soon. Looking forward to seeing more of your words.'

Party

"Hiya Gerry. How are you me old mate?"

"Fine, how about you?"

"Not bad, you know work, more work and then more work, that sort of thing."

"Look Sally and me are having a party on Saturday."

"When, where? Count me in, and hey, why are you having a party?"

"We're moving in together. It's sort of a coming together thing, her idea not mine."

Harry felt slightly uneasy.

"You and that lovely ex-girlfriend of mine are getting it together? Hey, that's great. So, what happens, are you moving in with her or is she taking her life in her hands and moving into yours?"

"I'm moving into hers, I'm not that stupid."

"Right, that makes sense. She'll take more care of her own place, yea, I get that. You lucky bastard."

"Yeah, well." Gerry sounded doubtful. "Look I just wanted to make sure it was okay with you, no hard feelings and all that."

"No, don't be bloody silly, Sally and me weren't meant for each other."

"Well, it's just that it was a bit tense there for a bit."

"Yes, I know, but don't worry. So, all this sounds serious, or is it just an easy way to get your leg over regularly?"

Gerry laughed, nervously, so Harry prattled on.

"Don't you believe it's cheap brother. It will not be cheaper, believe me. I've done it all before - remember. Moving in with 'em can be a very dangerous move, the rot will now set in. You are doomed but never mind, there's nothing you can do about that, so lie back and enjoy it."

"You seeing anyone?"

"Me, no mate, no women in my life at the moment, although I met one today who I plan to put on the list."

"Marked the bedpost yet."

"Yea, that's right, the notch is marked out on the bedpost already. No problem. Look I've got another call coming in, OK, I'll see you next Saturday. You never know I might bring her with me. OK if I bring a partner?"

"Be happy to see her."

"Yea, thanks, just wait and see what turns up with me. Look after yourself, and my condolences to Sally. Ask her how she could this to me. Cheers mate, see you soon, take care."

He spent the rest of the day giving his flat a monthly clean. The flat was a small, two-bedroom place over a hardware store. One of those really old-fashioned shops that sold everything, where you could buy just one screw if that was what you wanted.

It put him right in the centre of Hornsey and he liked that. He could walk to work. The shops were all around him and no taxis required to get home late at night. Cleaning the flat was not high on his list of priorities but he worked to a routine. It was better that way. A fortnightly purge saw the place restored, with that turned into a good clean once a month. With two marriages left behind he had few possessions and his cousin had helped him decorate the single living room, which was comfortable if not spacious. There was space for his books, a computer and two small sofas with a sound system and small TV hidden within a corner cabinet that was faced with a replica Warhol portrait of Marilyn Monroe.

The two children by his first marriage had flown that nest before he left. It was probably why it all broke up. He had married too young the first time, and they had spent years on the treadmill of work, children, house, garden, cars, pets, schools, work, children.... until one day he'd come home early from work. To find her running down the stairs pulling on her clothes, and puffing and panting coming from behind the locked toilet door. "Get him out," he'd hissed knowing it would never be the same again.

Later that day he sat down in front of his computer once more.

"A party, next Saturday. Lovely people, just your sort. He's a journalist. She's something of a researcher at the BBC. Lots of intellectual challenge, dress informal, wear those jeans again - if you like." He smilingly recalled that swinging backside on the car park staircase as he clicked on the 'Send' button. Could this be the start of something new?

* * *

Not having told him she had a partner, a party might be a problem. She wanted to go although she was not sure if she wanted to meet his 'intellectual' friends. Clever people frightened her; she always felt self-conscious, inferior, was not very good at small talk, and always managed to wear something entirely inappropriate. But Justin never questioned her movements very deeply, she could just say she was meeting Dee for a drink, that could turn into a binge. He would raise one eyebrow over his coffee the next morning and she would grin engagingly and that would be the end of it.

She sat looking at his email again. She had read it several times during the week., trying to read between the lines. Harry was such a funny name, especially for a copper. When he had told her, she had laughed and he had looked hurt. But she found Harry very sexy indeed. The name, not necessarily the man at that precise moment. Wear her jeans again! Bloody cheek. She spent the next ten minutes mentally browsing through her wardrobe, black bootleg trousers, skimpy top, short cardigan, and boots. She wanted to look good, then she wondered if 'intellectual informal' meant snappy or grungy. In which case she should wear her jeans. She wondered if it was a clue. Jeans, skimpy top, short cardigan, boots.

She disconnected from the Internet and clicked on My Documents, then opened the folder that contained her book. She read through the first chapter again. Then hit the page down button until she got to the point where she had left off yesterday, and began typing.

* * *

She heard the front door slam, Justin throwing his keys on the table in the hall, and the silence of him hanging his jacket on the coat rack by the door.

"You in?" His voice called up the stairs.

"Office." She shouted back. "Be down in a tick."

"I'll come up."

He kissed the top of her head. She leant back in her chair and smiled at him.

"I lost track of time, no dinner sorry."

"Oh, for fucks sake not again."

"Sorry. I said sorry. I just got going and didn't realise it was so late."

"Well, you can go for the bloody takeaway this time. No, in fact, don't bother, I'm going down the pub."

"Justin, don't. You've been out every night this week. I can cook now, won't take a minute to knock something up."

"You spend every night up here anyway, so what's the difference, at least at the pub people talk to me."

"I've nearly finished it, you know how important it is to me. I think it's good, I'm sure I can get it published."

"What like the last one?" He sneered the words at her.

"On second thoughts go to the pub, and you can go to the pub tomorrow as well because I won't be here. I've arranged to go out with Dee. I'll be back late so don't wait up."

"Fine."

Louise waited for the front door to slam. She wished the party was tonight. She wished she hadn't met Justin on the rebound. She wished she hadn't moved in with him so quickly after her divorce. She wished.

Buildings

The two men stood, leaning towards each other, so close that their bright yellow plastic site hats were nearly touching. Behind them the shell of a new building poked up towards the sky.

"Get a few skips on site, and fill 'em up. Make it look as if we are throwing away a fortune. When did the QS last come round to do a valuation?"

"Oh I dunno, must have been two or three weeks ago. Why?"

"Oh my son you have worked hard these last few weeks, I bet you were well ahead of the programme. Am I right?" Frank was wringing his hands, head down close to Paul's, his broad features puckered into a wide grin.

"Well yes, as it happens we were ahead of ourselves. I've been chasing up the Mowlem bloke to get other parts of the building released to us so we can start working." Paul's voice was quieter, slight slurred as if from too many years on the waccy-baccy. His slight frame hunched forward as he spoke.

"My son! What are you saying to me? This is music to my ears. Get round the site today and prepare a schedule of the work you've completed so far, and a list of the materials you've got on site. Then give it to me. Make sure you give it to me, you understand? Don't give it anyone else, don't keep a copy for yourself. Give the original to me." Frank's hands were about to start a friction fire. "You can write it on bog paper if you like. Just as long as it hasn't been used! I just want something to work from. Do you get my drift?"

"OK Frank, OK I get the picture. You are going to tell the client that we'd completed more than we have, so we can claim more than we should. Am I right?"

Frank grinned, tapping the side of his nose. "Least said Paul my son. You just do as I say and leave the detail to me."

"But Frank the main contractor must have a schedule of our work already. You have to send it in every week. You can only get away with so much. They are all over the site, all the time, they know what's going on." Paul shook his head.

"How long you been in contracting Paul? You are sounding like you just come out of school. Just listen to me, and keep it under your hat. You don't make money in contracting by doing a good job at the price you quoted to win the tender in the first place. The real money, often the only money, comes from what you can get away with, and how much you pick up on variations. Blimey if we had to rely upon the contract value alone we'd have gone bust years ago. You know that mate."

Paul tried to interrupt but Frank was now in full flow.

"I heard a little whisper about all this," he paused, dropping his voice as he glanced around the site, "so I just happened to forget to submit our returns for the past three weeks. So they don't have a clue, not really. Anyway by the time we submit the claim there'll be nobody who remembers what was on the site today. Besides, and this is the best bit, this is where the real money comes in, and that's with our suppliers. The chillers, the boilers, the air handling units, the ductwork, the control panels, all of the big gear we are using has had to be cancelled. Right?"

"But Frank I've not confirmed most of those orders yet, we've still got plenty of time to complete that lot, and anyway most of the stuff is off-the-shelf. Not the ductwork I'll agree but..."

Frank held up his hand. "Stop Paul, you'll have me believing you in a minute. One small example, my friend, that says you are wrong. I've got a confirmation this morning from the boilermakers. They are nearly finished making the boilers for this job and they say the cancellation fee is worth half the contract value. Would you believe that? They want that much because they say the boilers now have to be broken down and rebuilt." Frank laughed, "well that ain't strictly true, we have agreed to share the costs and the profits with 'em. It means we've already made 25% more on that deal than we hoped for. See what I mean Paul? Those stupid bastards don't know what's going to hit 'em yet. And I want to make sure they don't. Not until we are much further down the road. If they get an idea that costs are really going to soar they might cancel our contract and get someone else in. We don't want that, do we?"

As Frank strode away to meet and jovially slap the main contractor's manager on the back with a loud, "Hello Brian, are you coming to our golf match next Tuesday?" Paul realised why he was content to remain an engineer and not get involved in contract management. It was a minefield.

* * *

"Morning guv, cold enough?" Paul sniffed.

"You bet, here, there's been a bloke around asking for you." The gate guard pulled himself up straight, flexed back his shoulders, stuck thumbs into the top of the thick leather belt running round his fat gut.

"Oh yea, what'd you tell him? I'd been nicked by the Old Bill."

The guard hesitated, looking away uncertainly, before swinging back to laugh at Paul.

"Naw, I just said, like, I didn't know who he was talking about, know what I mean?"

"Yea, I know, like your grandma's been fucking the milkman all these years. Thanks mate. If they's asking chances are I don't want to know 'em. What did he look like anyway?"

"Short little greaser, loads of gold on his fingers, pulled up here in a Merc, one of them sporty jobs. Just wound down the window and shouted at me. Looked like a bleedin spic to me. I thought to meself, 'oy oy, here's one to watch, one that our Paul won't want to take home to his missus. Know what I mean?"

"Thanks mate, really good of you. If he comes round again get a skip lorry to dump on him, or better still we'll see if we can pump a bit of concrete inside his motor!"

The guard laughed as Paul walked towards the staircase, to climb up inside the building. It was that bastard Mungo, second time in a week. It was getting serious. Paul didn't know how to handle it all. He owed Mungo a lot of money. Too much money. He'd have to work something out.

The building was slowly taking shape. Dark concrete was being clad with wall lining, pipes and cable trays snickered across the ceiling. Climbing to the second floor he pushed open the door of the Portacabin. Noise, smoke and smell hit him in the face.

"Morning Sarah, and how are you this fine day," he leered across at a young girl who shook her carefully dyed pink-bleached hair at him as she sat at a battered wooden desk, pushing paper into envelopes.

"OK Paul, and yurself?" her Glaswegian rasp destroying any illusion looking at her had given him. You did not get randy with a voice like that. Just imagine, 'what are you doing tonite then Jimmy'. 'Eh, me, nought why?' 'then get up the hospital and get this fixed.' Blood, gore, deprivation and bloody thick. Who were these people? Ah well, so it was not all bad, thought Paul as he laughed to himself. Hark at the pot calling the kettle black! Was he any better than any other loser? Not at all. He got pissed, he couldn't go a day without the wacky-baccy. He took another quick look at Sarah. She might clean up nice.

This contract was coming to an end. It was a shell and core job, a block of offices in the city built by a property company who were now looking for tenants. Paul's team had installed all the basic services, plumbing, electrics, sewerage, air conditioning, fire protection and public lighting. They were never comfortable jobs as the building-services crew moved in as soon as the builders had put together the basic framework. In this case Paul had supervised the installation of all the main services to a restaurant on the ground floor. He'd also been told to install underfloor heating and ventilation. They'd been working away quite happily until the architect changed his mind. To be fair it wasn't the guy's fault. The developer had found a possible tenant who had raised just two objections. They wanted the catering area on the ground floor, not ten storeys up looking over Regents Park, and the air conditioning was now to be fitted in the ceilings.

As a result the developer's representative, a smartly dressed ex-public schoolboy, had haughtily addressed a contractors meeting with, "Don't want staff complaining about too much warm air blowing up their skirts. And we want a restaurant without a view. Up there they'll never get them back to work in the afternoon, and besides most of them are young girls, and they all seem to smoke, they'll want somewhere to chat and puff. Better they do that on the street. I'd put the canteen on ground floor, at the back, and get as much natural ventilation in as you can. This is no longer a fully air-conditioned job. I want the cheapest system we can get away with."

All that seemed reasonable unless you've just installed several hundred metres of 100mm pipe vertically from bottom to top of the building, and had ordered ductwork to fit under the floor, and were now being asked to turn the whole building upside down.

"All this don't come cheap you know Frank," Paul had said to his boss. "Besides it hurts when you've done a good job, taken time and trouble to get it all looking nice and tidy and its all got to be ripped out."

"Don't worry my son. We'll have a good holiday out of this lot. Variations to contract my son. Make sure you log every minute, record every item used, and ignore or spirit away anything that looks like it can be used again, and all the time keep smiling. We'll be called the smiling assassins." He laughed loudly at his own joke as he waved goodbye.

One Ex

He couldn't miss her, she was striding up the street towards him. Why did his heart jump whenever he saw her? It was all over, had been for ages, and besides they really had very little in common. Why was she still bugging him after all these years? He thought about turning tail and walking away from her, fast, but decided to stop and talk. After all that's what he really wanted to do. She was, no, she had been, the love of his life.

"Well, hello. How are you?" Harry looked down at the diminutive figure, whose elfin face was beaming up at him.

"I'm fine. Busy but happy enough, y'know, and you?"

He shuffled his feet uncomfortably, "it's been hard trying to put it all together again."

She snorted, "Well, we all make mistakes."

"Yes, it's just that I seem to make more than most." His mind raced, wanting to make a good impression, while fighting back the urge to say, 'and besides I only married on the rebound because you'd told me it was all over between us'. He kept quiet as Tanya spoke again.

"You make the choices in your life. You decide on the pathways to follow. If it's not right, well, you can change it." Her voice had dropped in tone, her face now serious.

"And you Tanya, how have you been?" Harry struggled a smile.

"Oh, I've not been well, nearly collapsed last week but went to see my kineologist. He is absolutely marvellous. He managed to sort me out straight away."

"So, what was wrong?" Harry changed his weight to the other foot, supporting his face on his hand, knowing this was going to take some time.

"Oh, I ate some mushrooms last week. Bought them from the supermarket, just ordinary organic chestnut mushrooms, y'know. Well, within a few minutes I just felt awful, really bad. Obviously I rested. But that was no help," she paused, taking a deep, even meaningful, breath before continuing, "you know that allowing the body time to recover from any allergy or illness is the right way. You do know that, don't you? It's important that everyone knows what to do in the event of an attack. Even an ex-husband."

He managed a grimace, "Sure, yes I know. You have told me before. So, what happened then?"

Tanya gave him one of her looks, "No need for that tone. I felt dreadful. Really bad. I had a contract to finish off for Chelsea but just could not manage to finish it that day."

"But you recovered OK?"

The look came again, coupled with a sigh, "I rang Charles and he agreed to see me right away. He really is so marvellous."

"How much did that cost?"

"What does that matter. He works miracles. He is worth every penny. Besides it was only £50, which is peanuts for what he achieved."

He shifted to the other foot, glanced up the street towards the supermarket, "What did he do?"

"That's the marvellous thing. He doesn't do anything. It's all done by him relating to the body. You don't play any part in it at all. He just puts his hand on your arm and asks your body questions."

"Great, what questions did he ask yours?" His tone was laconic. She was not amused.

"Listen it works! That's what is important. More cynical people than you have been helped by Charles. They keep going back to him."

He was tempted to ask why they should have to do that, but was interrupted as she streamed onwards.

"Within minutes he'd found it. The liver. That was it!" she exclaimed.

"So, what did he do then?" he asked.

"Well nothing. He doesn't do anything. The body cures itself. He just points out what is wrong."

"Sounds good." He really meant; sounds like good business for Charles.

"He found the diagnosis in a book or rather the body told him which page to turn to in the book."

"Hold on, how did the body tell him which page to open in a book?" Harry asked.

"He just said the body wants me to open this book, here on the shelf, and open it at page 325 and there it was, Liver Complaints." She beamed up at him.

"And now you feel better?"

"Well much better than I did. It will take time to recover fully." The serious tone, the lowered voice had returned.

Harry too spoke quietly, "What treatment was suggested?"

"Mineral water." Tanya spoke firmly and confidently, head thrown back in defiance.

"I'm glad you are to be sorted out." He paused, considering his next reply, before, "Marcus seems to be getting his act together at last. His web sites are looking really professional."

The voice lowered itself again as she gazed into the distance, "Yes, but it's only skin deep. He really is very depressed."

"Really? I emailed him several times this week. He seemed quite bright and cheerful." Harry knew his exasperation was beginning to show.

"Well, that's it then. I expect we'll see each other on Saturday." She was again perky and bright.

"Saturday, why?"

"Well I hear you are going to Sally's joining together party. God knows why she's inviting that waste of space into her home beats me, but I expect she'll learn."

"Oh, right. How do you know Sally?" The thought of spending an evening in the same room as his ex-wife and her girlfriend was too much to bear. "I didn't realise you knew her."

"She used to come to our Women's' Group, remember? Don't expect we'll see much of her from now on, pity she was a nice girl."

"Just because she has decided to be normal doesn't stop her from being nice!" His voice was now raised. This was going to muck up all his plans.

"It's a lesson I should have learnt about you years ago. You'll never learn because you never really listen. See you Saturday."

She pranced off down the road.

He noticed the supermarket doors had just closed.

Back home he sent an email, 'Louise; Plans changed for Saturday. Probably can't make it. Be in touch. Sorry.'

Crematorium

It still looked like a council yard, despite the large plastic direction signs and white lines painted over the decayed tarmac. As the car pulled into the yard they saw a shabby collection of low buildings squatting under the shadow of a railway line surrounded by bays full of salt, sand and road signs. Parking in a rectangle marked 'Visitors' they walked into the Portacabin luridly declaring itself to be the 'Head of Services'.

Squeezing past a photocopier through a door marked 'Reception' Paul found the ultramarine of these signs already beginning to grate. A young girl smiled, "Mr Trubshaw is in conference at the moment, would you like a coffee?"

"No luv, I hate waiting, we'll be in the car outside, give us a wave when he's ready." Frank pondered his way back to the car, followed by Paul.

"I hate all this," hissed Paul.

"So do I mate, but we've got to play the game, this is privatisation, remember. It's not like the old days, when these geezers had a job for life, knew it, and didn't care a stuff. Now, they have to work for a living. Well, they think they do. For us it's more bread and much more butter. Play up to the silly sods. You can handle the job, can't you?"

Frank paused looking directly at Paul. Something was happening, he thought, this guy used to be the life and soul as well as being a bloody good engineer. These days the sparkle had gone, he was no longer there with a quick reply, no sharp and witty riposte, as once as he had been. Someone said he was off the wacky-baccy, if that was true no wonder he feeling off colour.

Paul sighed, "Yea, sounds like the job's a doddle, although why they want to put air-conditioning into a crematorium beats me."

"No, it's more than that, they want heat recovery from the cremator as they burn up the bodies and to use that heat to warm up the chapel and the rest of the building. Sounds like a good idea to me." Frank licked his lips.

"Sounds a bit gruesome to me, you mean the last body pushed in the machine is warming up the next congregation, that's gonna cause a stir when Miss Do-It-Right finds out, but yea, I can make it work." Paul slumped back in the seat.

"Make it work, you gotta do more than that my son. You gotta persuade these silly sods that it's the best idea you ever sodding heard of. If this works we can sell this around the country. Cremation is big business, we're all potential customers, ain't we? I never realised before, but they are money, real money, and we can get some of that if we play our cards right. Looks like we're on." Frank pulled himself out the car.

The little receptionist was frantically waving at the window. Frank and Paul were ushered into a room. Across one end stood a large black desk from which ran a long black table, forming a 'T' shape. Black cupboards and filing cabinets lined the walls. Certificates were posted on the wall behind the desk. Paul peered at them, out of academic interest. Most were City & Guilds certificates in Business Administration. Paul sniffed and looked at the short man standing behind the desk. He was wearing a double-breasted green suit, a wide tie with a huge knot tied loosely around his neck. Paul noticed, with some interest, that the tie never moved as the little man's head twisted from side to side.

"Good morning, I'm Mr Trubshaw, Head of Services." The little man waited for their murmur of approval. "I've called you in to discuss my idea of waste heat recovery at the crematorium. Do sit down, would you like a coffee, my secretary will see to your requirements."

Without waiting for their response he sat down abruptly and began reading the papers on his desk.

Frank and Paul mumbled to the girl, who carefully wrote; white no sugar x 2, on her dictation pad before leaving them alone.

Mr Trubshaw continued reading the papers on his desk, twitching occasionally and twirling an oversize fountain pen along the margins. A tick here, a grunt, twitch, move paper, tick again. Not once did he glance up. Here was a busy man, making the most of all his available time, a new entrepreneur making the most of his privatised powers. Frank and Paul looked at each other, with just the hint of a smile playing on their lips. Neither man said anything.

Suddenly Trubshaw pushed the pile of papers forward on his desk and produced a signature with a flourish. Having done so, he sat, body taut, staring at the page for several seconds.

"Yes, that should do," he murmured, "Right gentlemen, thank you for coming, let's get down to business." He paused, looking hard at each of them in turn.

"I shall outline our requirements and then hand you over to our Mr Jackson, Head of Engineering Services and our Mrs Beech, Head of Bereavement Services. They will take you to the Crematorium, show you the present installation and we shall then invite you to submit your proposals for consideration. You will understand that this is to be regarded as a cost-benefit exercise. From our own figures it is clear that we can expect considerable savings for our Council Tax-payers with this scheme."

He paused again. He spoke in a clear East London accent, real Estuary English complete with glottal stop, but his humble origins were overlaid with just a veneer of 'posh'. Frank looked into Paul's eyes, and then glanced quickly away. Both men were on the edge of bursting. Trubshaw was turning into a caricature.

Frank coughed, "Mr Evans here," he took breath, for effect, "Mr Evans is our finest design engineer, which makes him, even though we say so ourselves, one of the best in the country. You will know us by reputation, I feel sure."

He stopped talking, stared very hard at Mr Trubshaw for several seconds, then took a deep breath before saying,

"As a company we are very interested in this project. The benefits to your Council are clear. More than that, there are obvious environmental advantages as well as cost savings. As for ourselves, we are," he paused again, "we are extremely interested because we pride ourselves in remaining in the vanguard of our industry. We would hope to persuade other crematoria to take advantage of our service. It should become a national standard. The concept you describe is brilliant. It will be our pleasure to work out the details."

Everyone smiled.

Trubshaw stood up, reaching across to shake Frank's hand,

"Well, thank you for coming, see my Secretary (he emphasised the title yet again) and she will arrange for you to catch up with my assistants, the Head of Engineering Services and the Head of Bereavement Services. I look forward to reading your report with some interest in the very near future. Goodbye, we shall doubtless meet again."

"Good job we know what this is all about, that jumped-up little sod was never going to be much help," said Frank as they slid back into the Volvo.

"Give him a break, Frank, he's enjoying all the power, and he's not really doing any harm." Both men laughed as they drove off to the crematorium.

No Party

'Fuck! Fuck!' She read the email and bashed her head against the screen several times.

"What are you doing?" Justin peered into the office.

She hit the disconnect button. "Oh, nothing, bad chapter, just letting off some steam."

"Well, I wouldn't, that machine cost a packet."

"Yes, I know, a small fortune, which you paid for. Although I thought you said it was a present at the time you gave it to me. Does if now mean you've changed your mind? Don't worry it's insured."

"I can't talk to you any more. I'm going out, said I'd meet Bill down the pub at six, we might go and see a film, then get a bite to eat, but I don't expect you'll be back before the early hours, will you?"

Fat chance. "No, I shouldn't think so, you know Dee."

"Okay, see you tomorrow then." He didn't bother to kiss her.

Louise waited for the front door to slam. She always seemed to be waiting for the front door to slam, she wondered if it was symptomatic of their relationship, him always leaving, slamming the door; one day she would leave and slam the bloody front door and then wouldn't he get a bloody shock. She looked at her watch, still enough time to send an email and find out why he was standing her up. She wondered whether he was sick, or suffering from cold feet, or just couldn't be bothered. She went back online, hit the New Message button and quickly typed out a short reply.

'You bastard! Either explain, pick me up at eight or never darken my inbox again.'

She hit the send button and held her breath, mentally visualising the email screaming down the phone line and landing with a loud thud in his inbox. She left the computer on and wandered into her bedroom and sat on the edge of the bed, then lay back contemplating the cobwebs loosely hanging from the light fixture. If he didn't reply by seven she would turn the computer off and phone Dee, who probably wouldn't be in or if she was would be in the middle of creating dinner for some unsuspecting victim that she had managed to entice into her web. The poor bastard would be too caught up in her skimpy clothes and the smells coming from the kitchen to notice her fangs, by which time she would have sucked him dry and spat him out the front door the next morning a shrunken husk.

Louise rolled over on to her stomach and picked up the remote for the television, flicking through the channels quickly through to a reality-sucks show, a quiz programme, a tacky American drama and the news, she switched it off. She couldn't bear the thought of being stuck in with only the prospect of Saturday telly to look forward to; she could rent a video. But that would mean a twenty-minute walk there and back, and possibly a mugging into the bargain. She could drive and hope there was a parking space, or she could go round to his house and demand an explanation. Or better still, she could suggest dinner instead of the party. If he was sick she could tend to his every need, but then again perhaps not, she didn't have a very good bedside manner, being of the 'take a pill and get out of my face' variety of nurse. Or, worst case scenario, if he was trying to give her the flick at least she would know once and for all.

She put the jeans on. Washed her face and re-did her make-up carefully, brushed her hair out, and puffed a bit of perfume on her neck. Not too much but just enough to let him know she had made the effort.

Margaret

"Just call me Margaret." She smiled, her lips thinly tightened against her perfect teeth. Smart, mid-forties, blonde hair stiffly curtaining her pale face. Nice woman, I'd give her one, thought Paul, but she looks like she's got more problems than I can handle.

"Mr Jackson will not be here this morning, but I can show you anything you may wish to see." The smile again, this time with a glistening hint in her eyes. She was getting more interesting.

Together they toured the building. It was an Edwardian slab. The red brick felt cold against Portland stone columns. Wreaths of flowers condensed against polythene wrappers. Silver foil 'MUM' and 'GRANDAD' surrounded by the wilting heads of doomed flowers, already turning brown at their edges. It all represented depression. Why should the only certainty in life be associated with so much tacky solemnity, thought Paul as he followed Margaret from room to room? He kept behind her tight bottom, wrapped in a dark blue skirt with two beautifully formed legs beneath. This woman was beginning to make him move. He had not felt like this for some considerable time. In fact he was beginning to wonder when he had last felt like this.

"What do you think?"

Paul was broken from his reverie. "Well, what do you think?" Frank grunted close to Paul's ear.

"Not bad, and we can handle the job as well." Paul grinned as Margaret turned to face him. She glanced away quickly. He was feeling really good.

"Yea, we need to fit a heat exchanger in the chimney, feed that back through to the domestic heating unit. Plenty of room in that plant-room, the one off the corridor at the back of the place where the coffin goes during the service."

"The catafalque," Margaret interrupted.

"Yea, there. Header unit up there, bit of ductwork into the chapel will give them warm air in there or we can put it into a pre-heat unit to heat up the water before it goes into the domestic boiler, it's all easy enough, it's up to you. Fancy we do a heated greenhouse out the back as well? "

He smiled at Margaret as she stepped back, turning towards the door.

"That will have to be explained again Mr Evans, slowly, in words of one syllable, so it can be understood by everyone. We'll not mention the greenhouse, if you don't mind."

"Don't worry, when he reads my report even Mr Trubshaw will understand what I mean, and I'll make personally sure that you understand everything about the system."

They all smiled, discreetly.

Frank drove back to the office, very fast and badly. Lurching acceleration and late braking did not encourage conversation and Paul was certainly not willing to break Frank's intense concentration. He sat in the passenger seat, alternately grabbing the door handle and pressing his right foot very hard onto the floor, while Frank hissed and snarled them to the grateful sight of the office car park.

Later that day they discussed the crematorium project over several large glasses of Scotch. It was the normal pattern. For some reason that Paul had never been able to understand Frank's wife lived in Wales. Frank stayed in London during the week driving to Wales at the weekend. Consequently he always wanted company during the week. Paul was expected to provide his fair share. At these sessions both men drank and smoked heavily and sorted out the problems of the world. They never talked about themselves, never mentioned their own problems, never revealed any innermost secrets. They were private men who together teased out the way forward for governments, for social and political history, for the future of their small business, but who kept their private nightmares to themselves. The drink helped, bringing the calm satisfaction that comes with impending oblivion. Eventually Paul would smoke a few joints while Frank crawled out for a take-away. More drink to wash it all down. Sometimes they would call for cab to take them home but normally both men would collapse over a desk until the cleaners arrived. It was a good life.

Party On

She didn't like driving in London at night, although the distance between Wood Green and Hornsey wasn't that far, it still freaked her out whenever someone looked at her sitting alone in the car as she waited for a green light.

She knew the road; she passed it quite frequently on the way to Dee's. In fact they had stopped off for a coffee at one of the many trendy little cafés nestling incongruously amid the fish and chip shops, Halal butchers and an Indian-run corner shop. She pulled up outside the shop, got out of the car and walked up to the door sandwiched between the old-fashioned hardware store and a garishly decorated craft shop. She peered at the row of names, and before she lost her nerve pressed the button alongside his name scrawled on a slip of paper, shoved haphazardly into the small plastic slot.

She couldn't tell by the expression on his face whether he was pleased or horrified. He certainly didn't look dressed to go out for the evening, unless grungy was de rigueur after all. He hastily pushed his shirt back into his trousers and swept his hand through his hair.

"Louise."

"Hi, I just happened to be in the neighbourhood." She paused, taking time to look at him with a critical eye, "actually that's a lie, I've come to see why you stood me up."

"Look come in." Harry shuffled to one side in the narrow hallway, waving one arm like a traffic cop on steroids.

He led the way up a flight of dingy stairs, into his flat. She was pleasantly surprised to find it neat and tidy and for the most part, clean. A few dirty dishes littered a coffee table in front of small, comfortable sofas.

"This is nice."

"Yes, it does for me. Coffee?"

"Oh, yes, ta." Louise plonked herself into one of the sofas. It was as comfortable as it looked.

He disappeared into the small kitchen. She listened to the noise of him filling the kettle.

"I didn't stand you up really, you know." There was a pause. She didn't respond. "I can explain." His voice was now quieter, did she sense a plea in his tone?

"Go on then." Her voice was firm and authoritative, even though she felt a mild twinge of guilt as she thought of Justin.

He stood in the doorway, "I bumped into my ex-wife outside the supermarket, and she just happened to mention that she would be going to the party too, an awful coincidence that I felt I couldn't deal with at the moment."

"I thought you were on good terms with her."

"Yes, sort of, but it's still rather painful. I could have handled it, but the person hosting the party is an ex-girlfriend of mine. It appears that the two of them discovered each other at some women's group and have become pals. You can imagine the scenario. I do feel a bit guilty about it, because the ex-girlfriend is going out with my best mate now, the party is to celebrate him moving in with her."

"Have you told him you're not going?"

He moved back into the kitchen and came out some moments later carrying two mugs. He sat on the identical sofa on the other side of the coffee table.

"No. I thought I'd make up some excuse tomorrow. He probably won't notice, they've got loads of people going." He sipped at his cup of coffee, pulling his lips away quickly as he realised it was still far too hot to drink.

"Shame."

"Yes, but he'll understand. I can always say something came up." He grinned at her, inanely.

She silently reached for her coffee.

"Anyway," he said, "how did you know where I live? This is serious stuff. If you know, then the taxman must know, the butcher, the baker and even that dumb blonde I met last week. OK, OK, drop the dumb blonde. I did."

He wondered why he always tended to babble when he was nervous.

She scrutinised him carefully. "Why do men think blondes are dumb?"

He sighed, ruffling his hand through his hair. "There really was this dumb blonde in my life for a short while. Just one evening in fact. We went out for a drink, nothing more. We go in my car, so I pick her up from her place. I play the gentleman, like you do and so I rush out in front of her to open the car door; the passenger side naturally only to look up and find her standing on the other side of the car by the driver's door. I look over the top of the car, and say, "Do you have the keys?" She stares at me, and Harry's voice raised an octave, as he mimicked, "No, this is your car." So, I say, "I thought you were about to drive." She looks perplexed, "No, I can't drive." He raises up to a high falsetto again, "Shall I come round that side then?"

Louise was impassive as Harry fumbled for words, "OK, it was funny at the time, and maybe the first time she was confused - maybe overwhelmed by my boyish good looks - who knows, but she did it again as we left the pub. And, anyway, why are we talking about her. She was dumb, that's all. Dumb because she wasn't my type and I wasted time with her. It's not important is it?"

Oh God, he told himself, just shut up

"Calm down, I just want to know why I was stood up." Louise remained in control, quiet but firm.

"I told you. I saw Tanya outside the supermarket. I discovered she was going to Gerry and Sally's party as well and I couldn't face it." He sounded tired, defeated.

"That's it?"

"I just panicked I suppose." This woman is feisty but I do like her tits.

"I suppose that will have to do."

Hey, this is cool, he thought, this woman's up for it.

"What shall we say came up?" he smiled into her eyes.

"Hold on a moment. I'm here to moan at you, not to make another date. You invite me to a party then crash me out. Now you tell me some cock and bull story about an ex-wife having screwed around with an ex-girlfriend of yours who is about to move in with your best mate. What's going on here? Is this a real cruise or just an ordinary swap shop?"

She reached for her coffee.

"That sounds like a great idea. One enormous gang-bang. I'd be up for that. How about you?" Harry laughed.

"Come on, get real. Are you seriously suggesting that I should get involved in an orgy with a man I have only just met and a bunch of weirdo's I have never seen?"

"Well, put like that you may have a point, the weirdo's I mean. They are all a bit strange. Perhaps we should wait for a while, they may improve." They both fell back in their sofas smiling at each other.

"Answer the question. How do you know my address?" he asked again.

"It's not important. I'm here now," she said. "Wanting to know why I was stood up by a jerk like you. I demand an answer from you - jerk!"

He sat back, saying nothing.

"Come on. I deserve a proper answer." Her voice was insistent.

"I told you the truth. I saw Tanya outside the supermarket. I discovered she was going to Gerry and Sally's party as well and I couldn't face it."

"That's it? That's all I get for a 'push off' email that leaves me feeling like a fool?"

Her tone had changed, the quiet smooth voice coming with a cutting rasp. "Doesn't sound like much of a deal to me. Just because you can't handle it I get the brush-off. Without even a second's consideration. How does that make me feel? So, your wife is important to you. Is that it? Perhaps you thought you'd go to the party by yourself, try to woo her over, is that it?" She was bolt-upright, hands now firmly holding on to the coffee cup as she warmed to her rebuke.

"Whoa. Can we stop all this? That's not the way it was. You're right. I apologise. I got it wrong. I should have thought about it, about you. But I didn't stop to think. I just panicked I suppose."

"I suppose that will have to do. Fat chance that I have of getting anything more." She stood up and moved across the small room to stand in front of the Marilyn Monroe painting.

"Is this the way you like your women? Dumb and blonde? You seem to have a penchant for blondes," she asked.

"Yes. No. Now hold on a moment. Marilyn was not dumb. She was seriously misused. Her story is one of the great tragedies of this century and," he added, "she was real crumpet."

"So you tell me. And I probably will agree." She turned her back to him, standing face the painting, legs slightly apart, the muscles in her legs tensed, as she thrust her hands down into the pockets of her jeans. He imagined taking her right now from behind.

She spun round quickly to face him.

"What are you going to do to make it all up to me?" she said.

He hesitated; reaching forward to take another sip of coffee then characteristically swept a hand through his hair as he wondered what to say.

"You tell me?" he said.

She remained silent, her large green eyes questioning until she said.

"I don't come that easy brother. You made the balls-up now you persuade me that the next offer can be relied upon and will be to my taste." She leaned over him, hands still in pockets. He noticed a small mole on her face and wanted to touch it.

"What do you like?" he asked.

She remained silent, her large green eyes questioning until he said.

"Football on the telly tomorrow night. Couple of beers, takeaway from downstairs, bit of a cuddle on the sofa. Will that do?"

"I don't like football much and I have a confession to make…" Serves him right she thought. "I have a partner at home, a disinterested one I will admit, but all the same a partner."

"Oh." He paused, looking straight into he eyes. "That does complicate the matter."

"Yes, I suppose it does, but on second thoughts perhaps not." Louise answered, looking at him in a sideways fashion.

"Does he know you're here?" He didn't fancy an enraged husband turning up on the doorstep.

"No, of course not."

"Would he mind if he knew?"

She frowned. "To tell you the truth I don't honestly know. Probably not. I met him on the rebound; he worked for the firm of solicitors I used for the divorce. Charming, good-looking, intelligent, prospects, that sort of thing. I had just dragged myself away from a compulsive gambler, liar and misogynist, he seemed to be the answer to my prayers."

"So you're on your second relationship, and there I was thinking I was an old reprobate trying to lead an innocent young thing up the garden path."

Any more surprises? He was beginning to like her more and more. The married ones were always less trouble, they tended not to hang around long, all they wanted was an illicit screw and they were content to return to the loving arms of hubby, no questions asked.'

"No, I do have an ex-fiancé though, but that was when I was much, much younger, a university romance that didn't survive the big bad world."

He sipped his coffee thoughtfully. It all slotted into place now; her abrasive manner towards him and probably men in general disguised a deep insecurity. Looks like he had met his soul mate in the insecurity department then. He had a deep distrust of women that probably matched her distrust of men. He decided to switch tactics. The heavy chat-up lines and innuendo's would have to go. He was out of practice in the romance department, although once upon a time he had been very good at it. He had pulled out all the stops for his first wife, Tanya, not in a contrived way it was just the way he had been then: flowers, candlelit dinners, the works. When she eventually left him, after a string of affairs, for a woman, and how was he to challenge that, he had lost his way for several years, eventually marrying a woman he never should have married. She had known, as he did, that he constantly pined for his first wife and it knocked all the romance out of him, he didn't have the heart for it any more. But for the first time since then he felt the first stirrings of those old romantic yearnings.

"Is it over, that's all I need to know. I can't go through all the trauma of seeing a married woman and not know where I stand. If it isn't over and this is just a little dalliance on the side then I have to tell you, at the moment all I could manage in that department is a one night stand, end of story. Basically, I need to know if this is going anywhere." For some reason he felt the need to be perfectly clear, to put his cards on the table, do or die, kill or cure.

She was taken aback by his candour; somehow they had jumped from a mild flirtation to discussing the possibility of some sort of a relationship without the usual run-up, and she wondered whether she should have opted for a night in with a video after all.

"Actually, and this may sound impulsive, but as from this moment, yes it is." She heard the words coming out of her mouth, felt her lips forming the syllables but it was as if someone else had said them.

There was a long pause. They looked into each other's eyes, faces impassive, bodies very still.

"Right, you can move in tomorrow. Have you got a lot of stuff, or will you be content with just clothes and personal items. I've got everything, fridge, cooker, all that sort of stuff, bed…"

"My computer, is there room for my computer? I will need that."

"Sure." He couldn't believe what he had just suggested; furthermore he couldn't believe that she had just taken him up on it.

"Can I sleep here tonight? I can't go back, not now I've made my mind up. If I can stay here until Monday, I can get my stuff while Justin is at work and leave him a note explaining. I can't stand the thought of a huge row, and all the unpleasantness."

He hoped if she ever moved on from him that he would at least deserve a little bit of unpleasantness.

"Let's have a proper drink." He got up, walking around the room for several moments before, "We need a drink. A bloody good long stiff drink." He soon emerged from the kitchen carrying two glasses and a bottle of wine.

"Hey, red wine. Is that all I get from you? Is there no champagne?" She was on her feet, beaming at him.

"Only red wine she says when I offer her the finest wine...." He held the bottle up high, "This is the best wine my good English lady. This is the fruit of the Gods."

He wondered as he watched her over his glass whether he should go for broke. He contemplated his options. Why would she have turned up on his doorstep. He raised his glass up high.

"We are mad. Completely and utterly insane. You know that, don't you?"

She nodded.

"We meet, we like each other. I am just getting to know the look of you, to find my way around you visually so to speak, and wham," he hesitated, "I have a house guest." He gulped back a great mouthful of wine and refilled their glasses.

She had been looking intently at him, following his movements, raising her glass, sipping at the wine. Now she sat down.

"Tell me about yourself, now, everything." She murmured into her glass.

"Not much to tell really. I've been buggered about by too many women, and all their crap has left me with a shell of a life. No real money. Fine, I have a job. It pays reasonably well. I can do most things but marriage brings much more."

She frowned.

"No, I mean it should bring much more. Marriage means two incomes in one life. Loads of money, put it into bricks and mortar, pensions and also you can have a good time. That includes kids and all that stuff. That was a good time for me. Then it all goes away. You get lonely, you feel hurt but most importantly you lose collateral. Money in the bank, cars, houses, furniture, everything - it all goes."

She shrugged, "And so?"

"So you get lonely. You get out there and play the field. You go looking again. Get caught again. Make mistakes again. Different mistakes, but still mistakes."

"So life's a shit and then you die. Is that the way it is for you?"

He chuckled, "No, I'm no shrinking violet nor am I a defeatist. I'll fight the bloody system until I drop. But...," and he threw himself down across the sofa, "but it is bloody hard work sometimes." He sunk more wine and reached for the bottle again.

"Hold on, you'll be falling over soon if you keep drinking so fast." She reached for the bottle and refilled her own glass.

They sat quietly, facing each other across the small coffee table. Neither spoke. Each reflecting upon the decisions they had just taken. Eventually he looked across at her.

"Are you sure you want to do this?" His voice was grave.

"No and yes." She kept her head down, watching the wine swirling round. "No I am not sure we should be doing this, and yes, I have determined to change my life. Don't ask me why but I feel changed somehow. Really we have barely said two words to each other but already I feel different. That's it. My life must change. I can no longer live with Justin. He's my partner, not my husband, by the way," she stopped, looking shyly across at him. Slowly they both smiled.

"Let's consider this carefully," he said "This morning I was alone and you were living with Justin. Now we are saying we will live together. That is a big step. I have to admit that it scares the shit out of me. This was not in my game plan. Twice caught, never again. That was the way it was going to be. Then you storm in here. Shout at me and then tell me you are going to move in with me. We are talking very big turkeys now. This is not wham, bam, thank you ma-am, there's the door ma-am."

"What are you saying; you don't want me here?" She frowned. Straight deep furrows across her brow.

"Yes I am. Not for this weekend anyway. This is a big decision. One we will not be able to make moping around here all the time. Where do you fancy going?" Standing up, he strode into the bedroom.

"What do you mean?" she shouted at his back.

"We'll go away somewhere. Spend the weekend together. See if it is likely to work before committing ourselves." His voice came back from the bedroom. "Don't you fancy a dirty weekend away then?"

"But I've got no clothes, nothing with me. I can't just go away, not just like that." Her voice rose even louder.

His head popped round the door frame, "So, it's OK to move in here straight away but if we are to be seen in public you'll need clothes. Is that right? Don't you think you'll need any if you stay here?" He paused, standing in the doorway looking at her, "This is all beginning to sound very contrived. You suddenly arrive on my doorstep - and how did you know my address? You arrive, unannounced. Then give me some story about an unloving partner, and then, just like that, you tell me you are going to move in with me. I'm not sure about all this. For now, I'm up for a dirty weekend but that does not come with any great cast-iron guarantee that I will not change my mind Monday morning."

She retorted immediately, "Five minutes ago you were talking a different tune. One night stands were out, you said. You wanted commitment, you said. And now what are you saying?"

He longed to rush to her, to hold her tight. Instead he quietly asked again, "Where would you like to go this weekend?" He didn't usually misjudge this sort of situation; he had spent the months since the break-up of his relationship with Sally moving from one one-night stand to the next. He knew she wouldn't have accepted his invitation to the party or bothered chasing after him if she didn't fancy him. He topped her glass up.

"It seems a shame to miss the party." She sat back sipping slowly.

"Depends what we're missing it for."

He cursed silently; he had got a massive dose of cold feet, he was simply hoping that a weekend on neutral turf would somehow calm his fear. Steady, steady, he said to himself, I must not bugger this up.

He hoped the wine would have strengthened his resolve, but it seemed to have weakened his instinct that this was the right thing to do. He was the one who had suggested it after all. He had said the words; you can move in here, and now he was trying to turn the tables on her, make it seem like she had foisted herself on him. True she had turned up unannounced on his doorstep, but that could simply have been the process of taking their relationship one step further in the natural order of things.

"I don't want to go away for a weekend. You asked me to move in with you and I said yes."

She was at once mortified and slightly relieved that he seemed to be backing down from his offer. But mortification won the day and she now felt honour bound to labour the point. After all in her own mind she had moved on, she had packed up her stuff, waved a final goodbye to Justin and was ready to begin a new life; he couldn't make her wait until he was ready, it wasn't fair.

He knew his instincts had been correct when she slowly put her glass on the table and leaned forward towards him. "Yes, I know, sorry. I'm confused. I'm not ready for this. I need more time. I was being impulsive. For once in my life I wanted to take the bull by the horns and do something really dramatic. Perhaps I'm too old for drama, I don't know." He sat down again. "We haven't even had a good kiss. How are we going to jump into bed with each other without all the preliminaries… the foreplay, the run-up."

"Why don't we go to the party, get blind drunk, come back here, go to bed and see what happens in the morning."

"Why don't we got to bed and see what happens now."

He was taken aback but continued, "Nothing will have changed. I think what I am trying to say is, that I need to know you aren't just using me as a convenient scapegoat. Quite frankly when we had lunch you seemed more interested in the food than me."

Louise laughed, shaking her head, "Well, I was but there is a reason for that. I gave up smoking a few weeks ago and food keeps the craving down, simple as that. I was very nervous, fancied you like mad, and I needed a cigarette desperately. Eating gives me something to do with my hands, food occupies my mouth, you know."

He got up slowly, negotiated his way round the coffee table and sat down next to her. He put one arm round her waist and lifted her chin with his free hand. The kiss lasted for several moments. When he let go of her, she was breathless, pink, her pupils dilated, her gaze slightly unfocused, there had been no resistance, no coy avoidance of his lips.

"Again," she said.

This time the kiss was intense, hard, and her hands, which had been lying inert in her lap, leapt into action. She undid the buttons of his shirt and pulled it loose from the waistband of his trousers. She ran her fingers over his stomach, which he instinctively pulled in and then over his chest and down his back pushing the sleeves off his shoulders. He lost the battle with his stomach and just let it go; he couldn't walk around with his muscles on full alert indefinitely, and she wasn't exactly poker thin. He was surprised at how firm her flesh was, when completely naked, she led him through to the bedroom.

As he lay back afterwards, her head resting on his shoulder, one leg over his, he could only describe it as blissful. It had not consisted of the frantic fumblings of two people unused to each other's movements and actions, as is so often the case when two people make love for the first time, everything had gone smoothly, like a well-oiled machine. He was glad that he had downed a couple of glasses of wine, it had taken the edge off his desire and he had managed to hang on until he was sure that she was ready.

"Well, here we are then." She pulled a hair on his chest.

"Yes, here we are, but what do we do now?" He asked, wincing slightly as she tugged a bit harder.

"Go to the party of course, " she answered, grinning up at him. "You can turn up looking well laid, and wipe the smirks off the faces of all your ex's."

The Party

The taxi dropped them off outside a large Victorian semi. Louise could here the beat of the music as she waited for Harry to pay the driver.

"Sounds like it's going pretty well." Louise commented as they got out of the cab.

"Let's go for a walk first, I need to prepare myself." Harry watched the taxi pull away from the kerb. He wondered if this was how the remaining passengers on the Titanic had felt when the last lifeboat was launched.

"No, we need to go in now, before the effects of screwing wear off. Any women looking for the signs will spot them at forty paces."

"God, I knew this was going to be a mistake." He took her hand and pulled her up the steps to the front door. He hit the door several times with his fist.

The door swung open. 'Harry!' A rather large overblown woman draped in a huge poncho, grabbed Harry by the shirt collar and hauled him in over the threshold.

She completely ignored Louise and disappeared with him into the throng of people lurking in the hallway. She heard him shouting over the noise, "She's my date, not my daughter, you silly tart, let me go!"

Louise gradually inched her way forward closing the door behind her.

"Hi, howya doin'?"

Louise smiled up at a man who towered over her, "American, you're American?"

"No, Canadian actually, but never mind, easy mistake to make. I just wish it didn't happen, we are bigger and better and on top of them."

"Sorry."

"Which side are you on?"

"Pardon?" she shouted.

"Bride or groom."

"Neither, I'm an interested observer. Anyway, I didn't know they were getting married."

"Well it's the same thing, living together. The noose has tightened. Poor bastard."

"Which side are you on?"

"Neither really, I'm more an interested gatecrasher with eavesdropping tendencies."

"Nice to meet you, sorry must mingle."

"Yeah, catchya later."

"Later." She smiled, moving towards a room that looked like it could be the kitchen in search of a drink to fortify her nerve.

"Louise, thank god." Harry grabbed her tightly by the arm and pulled her into a corner. "If you see her coming snog me or something."

"Who the fat lady or one of the ex's? Or is the fat lady?"

"Anyone who looks like they might know me."

"I could do with a drink."

"Over there." He nodded his head towards a table in the centre of the room. "Grab me one while you're there, will you?"

"Charming."

She picked up two glasses, examined them carefully to see if they were clean, took the only bottle that appeared to have anything left in it and headed back to the corner.

"Where are they then?"

"I don't know, I haven't seen either of them yet." He grabbed a glass and the bottle, filled it to the brim and downed the contents in one swift movement, wiping his mouth with the back of his hand. "I needed that."

"Do you think I might have a dribble?"

"Sorry. Here." He poured the last inch into her glass. "Sorry."

"Harry." This time the approaching voice was proprietorial, with undertones of whinge.

"Tanya."

"We thought you weren't coming." The small fair-haired woman looked up at him, examining his face carefully, and then eyed Louise, taking in the emerging smirk. "You look a bit flushed, you should lay off the wine. I was always telling him that when we were married, wasn't I Hal?"

It was the first time he could recall her calling him Hal. "Yes, I expect so."

"Are you going to introduce us?" Tanya turned slightly towards Louise.

"Yes, sorry, this is… this is…" For the life of him he couldn't remember her name.

"I'm Louise, remember." She poked him in the ribs. "The one with the most beautiful tits you've ever seen."

He coughed loudly. "Yes, Louise and this is Tanya, my ex-wife."

Tanya raised one eyebrow. "You never said I had beautiful…"

He knew she wouldn't be able to say the word, she had always referred to her boobs as bosoms.

"No, but you did have a nice bum."

"Oh for god sakes, you could always be relied upon to lower the tone," Tanya snapped.

"It wasn't me it was her." Harry looked accusingly at Louise.

"Anyway, have you seen Sally yet?"

"No."

"You'll never guess who else is here?"

He felt a small prickle of fear at the base of his spine. "Who?"

"Penny."

"Who's Penny?" Louise asked as she watched the colour slip from his face and disappear somewhere below his shirt collar.

"His second ex-wife, my dear, hasn't he told you. We're all here."

Not all, he thought, and perhaps he should wipe the smile off her face by completing the list. She hadn't been the only one capable of sleeping around. When he had discovered her with the third bloke tucked up in their bed, he had gone straight back out of the door and into the arms of the secretary he had been fending off for some months. They had seen each other for a few weeks prior to Tanya eventually leaving him and the affair had only ended when his inability to sustain an erection left them with absolutely nothing else to do.

"I said, are there any others here that we should know about'?" Louise shouted into his ear, "are you going deaf or just choosing to ignore me?"

He glanced across at Tanya who was watching him intently.

He gave her a wan smile, "Probably going deaf, it's the bloody music, it's driving me mad. I hate parties. Can never hear anything, can't say anything, meet a load of inane people."

"You never used to say that," said Tanya, "life and soul of any party in the old days. Are you getting a bit old for all this now? Perhaps you should be at home tucked up in front of the television with your slippers and a little white cat to stroke."

He shrugged.

"He doesn't have any slippers or a white cat as far as I know. Or have you been hiding something from me darling." Louise ran her hand round the edge of his right ear as she smiled down at Tanya.

"No, he never did like animals. The children always wanted a cat but he wouldn't allow it. Pity really, as I think all children should have an animal in their lives. Don't you think?"

"No idea. I don't have any kids."

"Harry was always very good with our children. I can't fault him for that. Except he did leave them at a very vulnerable age."

Harry gazed around the room. He recognised quite a few people. Everyone there was in the thirty going on forty range, most dressed in what they would all describe as 'smart casual' clothes. They probably all worked at some middle-income job. He didn't know everybody. The bird standing by the table with the floral dress and long woollen top sounding off in a loud voice just had to be a teacher. He turned to look at a group of men talking football beside him. They looked like the standard mixture. He guessed; bank or building society (the bald guy with a twitch), building surveyor (the moustache and green Pringle), a local government twit (the only bloke in the room with a shirt and tie) and the last had to be a fireman (short sleeved top, bronzed arms, trying to flex his muscles and stop himself from saying 'yeah' all the time). What the bloody hell did these people find to talk about? The teacher would be talking about her problems at school, so probably that group were all teachers and to be avoided. The men were into football, so were utterly dreary. Most of them appeared to know each other quite well. The few strangers would have a problem breaking in to conversations. What would they say to each other, 'Ooh hello I'm Vanessa, what do you do?' 'Well I fuck the arse off anyone I can find called Vanessa. It's your turn tonight. OK?'

"Anyway, it's good news about Sophie, isn't it?"

Harry looked at Tanya guardedly. "Yes, I think so."

"You don't know do you?" She treated him to a withering look. "He really is so awful. Used to be exactly the same with his parents. Unless I made him phone every Sunday he would just forget all about them. Your daughter, remember her, she's got a job at the BBC, in the research department." Tanya winced suddenly, bending over to clasp her side.

"Are you all right?" Louise asked.

"Yes, yes, it will pass. I get it all the time. Just one of the many crosses I have to bear." Tanya rolled her body from side to side.

"Yes," said Harry, "she has enjoyed ill-health for many years."

"You bastard!" Tanya shouted, suddenly agile, making the fireman and the building surveyor step back away from her. "If only you knew how I have suffered over the years. It's not my fault that I am not as strong as you are. If you'd had a little more concern for me then perhaps I wouldn't be in such a state today."

"I probably thought you had enough other men to look after you, and didn't need me."

"Don't you take the high moral ground with me. And as for your latest floozy, you'll let her down like you let everybody else down. She'll find out soon enough." Tanya sneered, as she turned away into the crowd.

"She's still got a soft spot for you then." Louise sipped her drink. "Floozy, what sort of word is that?"

"Bitch. What a bitch she can be. That was all for your benefit. You know that, don't you?"

"What do you want me to say. Let me see. I could say, 'there are no flames without fire' or 'I wish we were somewhere different?'"

'I would have done the same. That's what women do."

He suddenly laughed loudly. Even the teacher paused in the middle of her sentence.

"God, I want you. Let's have our cake and eat it."

"What do you mean?"

He slid an arm around her waist, pulling her towards him and nuzzled his lips to her neck.

"Let's do it again."

"What leave now?"

"No, let's do it here."

"What right now in front of all these people? Do you think they will approve?"

They held each other tight around the waist, hips pushing hips.

"Silly girl! We shall go upstairs. At the top of the stairs, turn left,; walk straight ahead and into the front room. Nice big bed in there."

"I suppose you would know that."

"Not in the way you think. She wasn't living here then. Her aunt left her this house after we split up."

"That was bad luck or bad timing then wasn't it. We'll see if your luck and your timing are better now, shall we?"

"I'll go first, slowly. You take your time, get a drink or something, then follow me up the stairs to delight." He nuzzled a soft kiss behind her ear.

They parted, with Harry moving away from the kitchen through the dining room, then the main living room, into the hall and up the stairs. He was unaware of the several pairs of eyes that were following his progress.

Several minutes later she negotiated her way through the legs and arms of several people sprawled on the stairs, followed his directions and tapped softly on the bedroom door before pushing it open. Harry was already under the covers his clothes strewn across the stretch of carpet between the door and the bed.

"God, you don't waste time do you?"

"Lock the door and get in here." He pulled back the sheets back to reveal his naked body.

"There isn't a key."

"Well, just put that chair up against the knob."

"Oi, watch it, no kinky sex please. I'm strictly a missionary position sort of a girl."

She dragged a heavy oak chair from its position by an enormous double-fronted wardrobe. "That should hold it, were you expecting visitors?"

"Quick before it goes down."

"Okay, okay, hold on, there's no rush. I want to make it worth waiting for.."

The music throbbed through the ceiling from downstairs, stopped and then the strains of 'Mama, told me not to come' filtered up through the floorboards. Louise, who had been about to take off her boots, stopped and began to sway gently to the music picking up the beat as the tempo increased. She slid one boot off and then the other, moving her hips from side to side as Tom's throaty voice hit a high note. She slowly undid the buttons of her Levi's rolling them down onto her hips and legs, kicking them away with one foot. Then she began to unbutton her shirt, letting it slide off her shoulders to the ground. Harry sat up in bed, transfixed. She rotated her hips as she reached up and slid the straps of her bra down each arm, turning away from him as she undid the clasp. Holding the bra up against her breasts she gradually slid the silky material backwards and forwards across her nipples, moving around to face him as she let the bra fall to the floor. She threw her head back, put her arms up over her head as the music began to reach its climax and let her hands slide back down her body. When she reached her knickers she hooked one finger in each side of the material and tantalisingly pushed one side down and then up again and then the other side, down and up again. She moved her feet apart, spreading her legs wide and bending forward until her fingers were nearly touching the floor, reached up and pulled the knickers slowly down over her thighs, and let them drop to her ankles. As the final note of the song was reached, she did a swallow dive onto the bed.

"I hope your timing is as perfect as that," she said breathlessly, resting her head on one hand.

"My god," he replied huskily. "You are wonderful, and to think I nearly blew it."

"No, I wasn't going to let you."

"I love pushy women."

"I wouldn't have classified Tanya as pushy."

"Don't, I can feel it wilting."

"I don't think so, is that better." She slowly ran her fingers gently up and down his erection, pushing the covers back she sat up and lifted one leg across his hips until she was positioned on both knees over him. She shuddered as he slid effortlessly into her.

"Oh, god, yes."

"Oh, Harry." Louise moaned, moving carefully up and down.

He slowly ran his hands from her knees up her legs feeling the tension in her thighs, then placing one palm on the flat of her stomach as he followed the movement of her body as she slowly raised up on him, again and again. The fingers of his other hand felt for the warmth of her breast. He gently rolled the erect nipple between his fingers as she moaned softly, head down watching his work. Slowly their tempo increased. She moved forward, widening her legs and rocked up and down as he hardened onto her nipple, thrusting his hips upward to match hers. His other hand moved down into her mound moving lightly along with her rapidly increasing moves. He raised his hips further, thrusting forward hard as she threw back her head and moaned, "come one, come on, go for it cowboy, ride on, ride on" until they reached a long gentle climax together. Finally spent she threw herself forward to kiss him violently.

The chair positioned at the door, suddenly rocked forward, hit the carpet with a dull thud, and fell sideways.

"…and this was Aunt Maude's room."

Neither Harry nor Louise moved, aware that a figure now stood by the bed. Not a word was spoken. No one moved.

"Am I too late?" the voice was gentle, even lilting.

"Yes, Penny, as usual." Harry replied just as quietly.

"Wish I'd known you would be so fast. I'd love to have been here. I saw you come upstairs, one after the other and I guessed. She has a lovely body Bramble darling."

"Bramble? Who's Bramble?" Louise's voice was at a low whisper.

"That's me. This is Penny. Another wife. Can you leave us alone Penny? Please."

Penny sat down on the bed, "I called him Bramble because he was always so prickly with me. Don't mind me please. I'm not really kinky. I've never done this before. I mean been there when, well you know, when two people have…. It was a lovely moment. I stood just outside the door listening to you both, and then I just had to come in to see you once I knew it was, well, once it was all over."

Louise slid backwards then rolled across Harry's chest to look at this intruder.

"A first for you was it. That's nice. What's the matter with you. Did you want to join in?"

Penny giggled, "Oh no darling. Bramble will tell you that I was never really into all that. I mean I loved kissing and cuddling all that, how would you say, all that stuff that goes on before but not sex itself. All too squidgy and messy for me darling."

"Thanks," said Louise, "you have really helped."

"Penny, please fuck off darling. Let's talk later shall we. This is not the time. Do you mind, please." Harry's voice was kind, even warm.

"Oh Bramble. Oh, OK I'll go downstairs then shall I?"

"Good idea sweetheart. Go and see if you can find any of that Pimms you like so much."

"Ooh Brambly you are so clever. I haven't had one of those for ages. Do you think they'll have some?"

"Sure of it. Find Gerry and demand he give you some, with cucumber and borage. Tell him not to forget the borage."

"Right. Yes. That's a lovely idea. Do you want one as well? I mean both of you."

"Yes please Penny. A big one," said Harry as Penny stumbled out of the room.

"I've just had one of those," sighed Louise. "What was she on?"

"Could be anything. She used to just smoke a little but these days it could be anything. She won't remember a thing later. Well, not much anyway. How about you, will you remember?"

Louise snuggled up to him, letting her fingertips run down the side of his face.

"Certainly will. Not even she could have spoiled that. The earth, as they say, wobbled my brain beautifully. That was bloody good. Fucking good."

They lay entwined for some time, wrapped in the warm duvet, lost in their own private worlds.

"I suppose we'd better put in an appearance before the wandering drug addict returns with the Pimms, god forbid." Louise stretched out on the bed, wriggling her toes contentedly.

"Do we have to, can't we just go back to my flat now?" Harry felt desperation creeping into every limb.

"Two down, one to go. I can't go without meeting the full set."

"I think this is tremendously unfair. When do I get to meet your mistakes?"

"I don't think you ought to meet Justin, he'll just beat you up."

"How big is he?"

"Huge, he plays football, squash, anything that involves a ball really, and he goes to the gym three times a week. I wouldn't go there if I were you."

"Oh, all right then, just a thought." He lifted up an arm, flexing the muscle. "Feel that."

"Puny," lifting her own arm up. "Try that for size."

He had to admit that they may not be bigger but they were harder and consoled himself with the fact that he could always hide behind her if it came to it.

"Right let's get this show on the road."

Louise leapt off the bed, retrieved her clothes and was fully dressed before he had even managed to lift himself up into a sitting position. She threw his trousers at him.

"Come on. I need a drink. Do you think they've got any food, I'm starving."

He turned to look at her. He was not sure he had the energy for this relationship if it was going to continue at this pace. He nodded wearily, wishing he were fifteen years younger. Perhaps he ought to start going to the gym. Then scrubbed the thought, he'd have to get fit before he'd even contemplate bearing all in front of the muscle-bound types that he knew frequented the fitness centre.

They negotiated their way back down the stairs and into the kitchen in search of drinks. Louise noticed a very thin woman glaring at them from the corner of the room.

"Who's that?"

Harry turned to look. "A full set, I believe."

"Well, watch out because she's headed this way."

Harry smiled broadly at the approaching figure. "Sally, how are you?"

"How dare you?" she hissed. "This is my house, that was my aunt's bed, she died in that bed."

"What do you mean?"

"I saw you. I was giving Penny and Tanya a tour of the house, and what do I find, you and her at it in my aunt's bed."

"Well, you should have said something."

"I am. Now."

"Look, I'm really sorry." Louise smiled warmly at Sally. "It was my fault, I dragged him up there."

"And who are you, the next soon to be ex-wife of Harry the serial husband?"

"No, I'm already committed as it happens."

"Oh, lucky you. Of course, he didn't want to marry me, did you Harry?"

He had wondered how long it would take for her to bring the subject of marriage up.

"I thought you were happy with Gerry. For Christ sake, you left me for Gerry, remember?"

"Only because you wouldn't marry me."

"Sally, don't do this," he pleaded.

Sally's eyes filled up with tears and she stepped forward leaning her head against his shoulder. "Harry, I love you, Harry. Please let's try again."

"Stop it! You're drunk, you'll only regret this later."

She lifted her head up and stepped back.

"I'm not drunk, and the only thing I regret is not killing you before I left, and now I am going to get drunk, but first of all I have to make an announcement."

"Oh Christ." Harry watched her weave her way through the kitchen and into the living room. A few seconds later the music stopped and the sound of her voice rang out.

"Can I have a little quiet please. I have something to say. Everyone be quiet, I want to say something."

Gradually the noise of conversation, laughter and the clinking of glasses and general movement dimmed into complete silence. Tanya suddenly appeared beside them with two bottles of champagne.

"Harry, open these will you, I think the big moment has arrived."

"No, don't." Harry grabbed the bottles and watched Sally through the door, he saw Gerry move to stand beside her and groaned.

"I would like to announce that I am still in love with Harry and I don't love Gerry and I don't want to live with him and I want everyone to go home." She put her hands up to cover her face, turned and fell into a chair.

Tanya turned on him. "You bastard, look what you've done now."

Harry watched the smile on Gerry's face slip away and decided that discretion probably demanded he disappear. Grabbing Louise's arm he steered her towards the front door.

"Hey, not now, this is just getting interesting." Louise twisted away from him.

"Come on, there's nothing we can do here now. She's drunk." He had seen Gerry's eyes searching the room, looking for him.

"No, let's go." He tugged at her arm as his eyes made contact with Gerry's.

Louise did not move as Gerry reached them.

"We need to talk," Gerry said as he turned on his heel and walked out of the front door. Louise and Harry followed.

The cold night air hit them as the moved out to the gravelled front garden with its obligatory blue pot. For a moment the two men just stared at each other, feet apart as if poised to strike.

"Right, let's get this sorted out now shall we. What's going on?" Gerry's tone was demanding. Harry shook his head.

"God knows. She's drunk, nothing more than that. She'll be OK in the morning." Harry glanced nervously towards Louise who said nothing.

"Bloody hell, we were getting it together." Gerry waved his arms back across the crowd in the house. "This place is full of people we invited to a party to celebrate our moving in together," he looked up at the sky, "but now it looks like it never really ended between you two." Gerry crossed his arms and stood back looking at Harry, who reached forward to touch the taut figure on the shoulder.

"Look mate, it wasn't like that. There's nothing going on. It's all over. I've got nothing going on with Sally. It's you and her now. My best mate with a lovely girl who I like a lot. But what do you want me to say?"

Gerry shrugged, shuffling his feet across the gravel. "Well it doesn't look too good for me now, does it?"

"She'll be all right. You know what she's like. Couple of drinks inside her and she always gets maudlin. That's all it is."

The other man grunted, nodded his head and turned towards the door where Sally stood on the threshold. Her eyes fixed on Harry as he took hold of Louise's hand and pulled her down the path. As they reached the pavement Sally called out softly, "Harry. Harry, don't go. Please don't go."

"You crummy bastard," Louise whispered, as they walked towards the main road to hail a cab.

"What do you mean?"

"You didn't behave yourself with her either, did you?' Her voice rose, as he turned away, arm outstretched to hail a passing taxi, which pulled alongside the kerb.

Inside the cab she looked at him again, "I'm right aren't I?"

"What do you mean?" The cab purred away.

"She's still got the hots for you.'

He hesitated, "I don't know what you mean?"

"Oh yes, you do.'

He nodded.

Louise whooped loudly, "I knew it.'

The cab pulled into Southgate Lane, accelerating over the rise. "We met one night. I suggested a meal. We had a good time and it just er… it just happened."

"When was this?"

He paused before muttering, "It was a Wednesday."

"I've got to give it to you. You have a definite way with women."

Moving On

Louise stared out of the cab window watching the pavement move past in one fluid grey streak and sighed. She didn't know why she felt betrayed. After all she'd had her fair share of liaisons. How many men had there been? She frowned, roughly calculating a figure in her head, trying not to recall too many of the details as she thought of individual names. Not one of them had lived up to her expectations. Admittedly being force fed a diet of romantic movies from the age of thirteen hadn't helped. But if Ali McGraw and Meg Ryan could find true love, on more than one occasion, why couldn't she?

Her heart had been broken at a very early age. His name was Jeremy and she was just ten years old. He was the first boy she had kissed. Chaste, damp kisses, snatched at odd moments during one summer holiday. They had met at youth club, and he'd her hand and lead her away from the main hall into a corridor of the school building. But it had ended as quickly as it had started. He dumped her one Friday night, getting his best friend to tell her he'd now got another

Shortly after this ill-fated affair, her father had taken a job in France, and then another in Germany. It was the most exciting time in her life. There were a series of teenage relationships, that had either ended in tears or because she had moved away. It was a transient life, people came and went, but friendships always seemed more intense because of the nomadic expatriate lifestyle. They were lived to the full in a kind of desperation to get the most out of them before they were wrenched apart.

She wondered if this was why her relationships with men seemed rather tortured, she would cling to them, stifle the life out of them until the men usually gagging for air would up-sticks and leave.

"What are you thinking about?" Harry asked as the cab slowed for a red light.

"Men, I'm thinking about men."

"What about them?"

"I think I might become a nun."

Harry turned in his seat to look at her. "You can't do that."

"Why not? I could dedicate myself to good works and not have to worry about stupid, fucking men any more."

"Do you want me to take you home?"

"I thought we were going back to the flat."

"Well, I thought…"

She stared at him in disbelief. "Oh, I get it."

"What do you mean?"

"Don't worry, I'm gone and you won't have to see me again. I can take a hint." She tapped on the glass partition, telling the driver to stop, jumping out as soon as the door catch was released. "I hope you and Sally are very happy together."

"You silly cow, get back in the lights are now green."

She slammed the door shut. "Piss off back to Sally."

The car behind them honked their horn and a head appeared from out of the driver side window. "Fucking get going." A voice shouted.

"And you can piss off back to Sally too." Louise shrieked, taking a few steps forwards.

The head disappeared and the car slowly negotiated its way round Harry's, the window now closed. Both occupants stared resolutely ahead.

"Get in."

"No." Louise crossed the road and began to walk away from the traffic lights. The cab followed behind slowly, the driver was clearly enjoying this encounter. Harry wound down the window, leant out and shouted, "I don't want to go back to Sally. I never wanted to be with Sally. I want to be with you. I'll take you back to the flat. I didn't mean that was it."

Louise increased her pace.

"No, Justin will be wondering where I am."

"Justin, since when where you concerned about him?"

"Well, he doesn't seem like such an awful proposition after the night I've just had."

"Louise, please, get in. I'm not going to ask again."

He knew it was the wrong thing to say the moment the words came out of his mouth. He watched her cross the road in front of him and begin walking along the pavement back the way they had just come.

He jumped out the cab, shouting at the driver to wait.

"Look you can't walk all the way home, it's bloody miles, you'll get mugged and at this rate I'll get picked up for kerb crawling."

She stopped. "Are you saying I look like a tart?"

"Get in the taxi."

Slowly Falling

Over the next few weeks Paul worked on the crematorium project. From his outline ideas draughtsmen drew up the detailed plans, while Paul checked with suppliers, preparing cost plans and programming schedules and pored over the vacuous detail of the Council's contract specification. Finally he was ready and spent an intensive hour taking Frank carefully through every part of the work. Private lives may have failed but as professional workers they showed a competence and dedication that ensured that the work kept coming to them, at the expense of their competitors.

During that time Paul saw Margaret several times and spoke to her on the phone nearly every day, carefully checking everything about the tender submission he was about to submit. With a strange sense of anticipation he slowly found himself looking for reasons to contact her, and was pleasantly content to find that she was happy to talk. Gradually they relaxed, enjoying each other as friends, allowing the conversations to move beyond work into their own lives. She had been married, that much he knew, but no more. Her husband had been an accountant, but each time they talked of relationships Margaret changed the subject.

Their talk was of the mundane, light-hearted but concerned. Both had a Friends of the Earth attitude towards the world, which inspired many of their discussions, leading to animated debate about hunting wildlife, especially whale hunting, to which they quickly found they were both totally opposed. They were both reluctant meat-eaters; she because her family had demanded she prepare flesh for them to eat, he because restaurants rarely included anything inspiring on their vegetarian menus. These conversations were not really debates but a series of statements, in which one would tentatively broach a subject, looking for a reaction from the other. They would start, diffidently,

"I don't know what to think about fox-hunting," one would say,

"No, nor do I, there are those that say it is necessary to keep down the population of animals that are really no more than pests."

A pause, then, "Yes, that may be true, but I read somewhere that fox-hunting is responsible for less than one percent of the fox-deaths in any year - so it's not very successful, is it?"

The long pause again, then Paul would often loudly voice how they both really felt with a, "Stuck-up bastards, trotting round the countryside as if they owned the bloody place!"

To which Margaret would reply, "But they probably do!"

Both would then collapse with laughter, eyes twinkling at each other, as Paul rested his hand gently upon her arm. Precious moments that slowly built together until they both realised they had a relationship neither wanted to end.

Yet the friendship remained static, not moving forward to closer contact, onward to passionate embrace or demonstrations of undying love. They were friends, very good friends, but neither was willing to take an irrevocable step, to make a definitive statement. Within themselves this failure to publicly demonstrate how they really felt towards each other led to some rather bizarre situations. Paul became increasingly belligerent about the inhumanity of his fellow men, pointing out failure whenever he could. Nuclear war, the countless unnecessary confrontations, the failure of the religious establishments, and much more, became the focus of his anger. This inner turmoil was born of his inability to express how he really felt towards Margaret. He was inwardly terrified of rejection. Here was a person to whom he could relate, yet how was he to offer her anything?

***

Paul had finally begun to understand that he had a problem with drugs. The problem was he owed Mungo for them. And Mungo seemed to be getting cross. He'd obviously tried to catch Paul at his flat, as the little old lady who lived upstairs had knocked quietly that evening, just to tell him that a very noisy man had called. Paul recognised the signs, the pot containing the grapevine he was giving tender loving care had lain smashed against landing of the fire escape outside his flat when he arrived home. "OK, thanks. I think I know who that was. A nasty man. If he comes here again, and I'm not here will you please call 999?"

She'd not been happy at that suggestion, hand to mouth, nervous glance, all of a quiver.

"It will be OK. Just dial 999. Say there is a strange man outside and you think he is trying to break in. You won't be lying, look what he did here today?"

Eventually she left, a small hunched figure, creeping back up the steps at the rear of the large Victorian family house, now converted into a number of separate flats.

Paul hoped that might keep him at bay for while. He owed Mungo money. Ironically it was not his debt that Mungo was after, but that didn't really matter, at least not to Mungo. Paul had been working on a large site, big block of offices near Liverpool Street station. Many of the workers were from Eastern Europe, Kosovans, Croats, Ukranians. Only one or two spoke English. One had asked Paul to get some drugs. Paul had held back, he didn't want to be a drug-dealer, but had been persuaded to act as banker. The men had given him orders, on slips of paper, that he'd passed on to Mungo. He'd never taken any money. The workers paid the same price as he'd have paid himself.

Moving In

Back at his flat Harry went straight into the kitchen to put the kettle on.

"I told you we shouldn't have gone to the party," he said, setting out two mugs on the counter.

Louise flopped down onto a sofa. "No, I think we should have. It was certainly an eye opener."

"That's a bit unfair. I didn't have any idea that Sally was going to launch into a swan song. Poor bloody Gerry."

"Poor bloody Sally more like."

"Typical." He handed her a steaming cup and sat down opposite. "You women all stick together."

"Well, I'd rather be a woman if that's what being a man means."

"I thought she understood. I didn't think she'd want it to be anything more than a screw."

"Women don't think like that. They don't screw. They invest their emotions. Even if it's a one night stand, they always hope it might be something more, except when they're pissed of course."

"Well, let's just say I was pissed and I wish she'd been pissed too."

"You weren't pissed, were you?"

"No, but I'm incredibly bored with this conversation and anyway, we hadn't done anything, and I don't want to know anything more about Sally, so I don't know why you're getting so upset."

"Me, upset, why should you think that? I'm seduced, taken to a mad party, where I'm ravished yet again, in full public view of many of your wives. Who do you think you are, the Sheik of Araby with a thousand wives"

"Hold on, I think you shared in some of that seduction process. I do protest Milord, she was wanting me to do it."

"What now? Again?"

"Standby, the Stud of the East is about to descend upon you, yet again, unless you can provide a really good defence."

"How about," she smiled, "it's late, you've had a busy day, and besides, little boy I think you've already had your fair share. Let's see what tomorrow brings."

Mungo

The door buckled, the sound of a vicious thud rang through the flat. Paul, in the kitchen, instinctively ducked before mouthing, "aw shit!" as he ran down the short hall and into the living room. He struggled with the handle of the fire escape door, swearing silently as the lock refused to turn. What was happening? This was supposed to be a bloody fire escape! Thud, thud! Again, the front door creaked against the onslaught. It wouldn't hold out much longer. Paul twisted the key in the lock. This was not the time to get temperamental. He needed to get through that door. He had to get out. There was a good chance that his life depended upon his getting out, and away from his apartment. There was a final crash, glass tinkling to the floor. The grunt of exhaustion, and a muffled shout, "Where are you, you bastard. I'm going to cut off your balls. I know you're in here. Come out bastard!"

Mungo! Now Paul knew he had to get away. He took a deep breath, looked hard at the lock, and murmured, "OK, this time." The key turned smoothly in the lock. He was quickly through the door, closing it silently behind him, and in a moment was down the stairs, over the fence into the next garden.

Behind him he could hear Mungo yelling at the top of his voice, as furniture was hurled around the rooms. He hopped over the next fence, and into the passageway that connected to the next street. Walking quickly, but not running, he didn't want to be spotted by one of Mungo's henchmen, who might be with him, he made his way towards the shopping centre. Once there he made for a Wimpy, sitting right at the back of the restaurant, close to the kitchen, he ordered a cup of coffee and a wimpy and chips. He needed time to think. Hopefully Mungo would not consider he'd be sitting in a Wimpy.

He'd better call on Gerry, he knew he'd let him stay there for a few days until all this blew over - or he found another flat somewhere.

He'd been too soft, too willing to help, and now look where it had got him. He could kick himself for his stupidity.

Gerry

"Is there any way to get out of this stupid mess?" he slumped forward in his chair and groaned. "I feel like a car leaving a wedding, behind me is a load of tin cans, in each can there's a problem and they are jangling my life away." His voice rose to a crescendo, and he bellowed as he jumped to his feet, "God! What are you doing to me? Why do I have to suffer like this, why, please tell me why I should be the chosen one?"

The shout fell to a whisper as he choked, tears running down his face. He reached for the bottle and drank.

Sally. What the hell had he been doing getting involved with her in the first place? Well, OK, yes, it had been a long time, and she had been willing, bit too much so for his liking really, but that would have worn off with time. She was a nice girl, just obsessed with Harry. Or was she? Was it just that she liked to make the decision? Had Harry given her the push? And so she had decided to pay him back, by publicly dumping poor old sympathetic, always there, Gerry.

Whatever, it was all over now. She was not coming back into his life, not as a lover anyway. Pity really. Her aunt's place was really nice, a great house for a family. What? He'd already got one of those, couldn't handle another.

Gerry stretched back on the sofa, swigging again at the bottle. What a week. Sally had thrown him out, and he'd lost his job. He was now to be called 'Redundant Man'. Nothing wrong with that, he deserved a break, a little time to sort himself out. He'd been working away for years. There was now time in his middle-aged luxury to sit and look around whilst he watched the redundancy payment he'd receive for half a lifetime of good and relatively faithful service slip away. He sipped again at the bottle, planning visits to the local Job Centre.

"It won't last for ever", he muttered to himself, "but who gives a fuck! Enjoy it sunshine, enjoy it. It's all yours, to do with as you wish! No-one else to get in the way."

He shouted the last at the reflection that stood before him in the mirror. He moved closer, staring closely at those eyes. What was behind that face, who was in that head? Who was he? Where was he going? Mid-forties, just dumped by a woman and the next day thrown out of the only firm he had ever worked for, where he had coasted along quite happily for years. Life had been a doddle, although he had worked for it, after all did they ever take into account the worry and anguish they had caused him? What about the McClellan project? Hey, could they have ever got through that little fiasco without him? One clear straightforward answer to that Gerry, my old son,

"No, bollocks to 'em, they were always a complete load of arseholes. Never did really like any of 'em, specially that Peter Mansfield, who the fuck did he think he was anyway, ignorant bleedin arsehole of a man. Be better off on my own. I don't need no-one," he moaned as he fell to the floor.

He woke later, alone in the conservatory. His head hurt. His collection of house plants looked as tired as he was. Gerry looked around the small conservatory, saying to himself, "Plants do have feelings, you know. They may not be easily recognisable to us, but is that their fault or ours?"

He paused, swaying back on his heels as he carefully picked up a glass of whisky and slowly sipped at its contents. Waving his arm in a wild gesture as he put down the glass he said, in a very loud voice, "We must recognise the destruction of the world in which we live will era-eradicate us, kill us, yes, it will be us what gets the chop, not the bleedin world, not the earth. That has survived far worse than we can hand out. It's had loads of tragedies during its 4,000 million year history" He paused.

"You can't get your 'ead round four thousand million bleedin years, can you? That is a really long time." He slumped down in a chair, breathing heavily as he took another swig of scotch. "And," he went on, looking around the room with a glassy stare, "and we must remember that we need pretty special conditions in order to live comfortably. I need plenty of this for a start," he said taking another drink, as he slumped back in the chair.

"You just imagine it. Just imagine you's sitting in a smoke-filled room without smoking yourself. Now, think about it, just sit there for a moment and think about this, 'cos it's important. Now, become aware of the smoke, breath it in,"

Gerry coughed, "feel how it makes your eyes sting, don't it, taste it on your tongue, smell it on your clothes."

He picked up the sleeve of his jacket, breathing in deeply. "Now, just imagine a world where all the air was like that, a smoke-filled room, where you could never breath in fresh cool air," he paused to take another swig of whisky.

"Well, we are not far away from such days today." He coughed, feeling the slimy result in his mouth. He swallowed, knowing he needed a drink, he was thinking too much.

His brain went on muttering. "We are what we eat." He coughed, spluttering into his glass, "Now listen, this is important. Take today, see we are eating processed crap all the time. Bleedin cardboard boxes with rubbish inside that's all you find in supermarkets these days. Isn't that right pretty green plant, we'd soon gobble you up wouldn't we? Then we'd say is it meat, or soya, or some other unidentifiable load of crap." He rose to his feet, shouting out loud, "It's all a load of crap. The whole fucking world is a load of shite!"

Falling back in the chair Gerry picked up a houseplant, a small cactus, covered in its own sheepskin coat, muttering, "We have vegetarians, who eat vegetables, we have vegans, who eat no animal products at all."

He rose to his feet, stumbled, and went tripping across the room, holding the cactus aloft like a winner's cup. "But no, you see, we don't seem to have a group dedicated to eating only the stuff that nobody wants. The shurplushes. You see what I mean? The seeds and fruits and all that stuff. Not that anyone would call you, little cactus, a surplus – more like a bleedin freak if you ask me. No, it's fruits and seeds and all the excess stuff I'm talking about, ain't it? All that stuff we can con from animals, like milk. What a bleedin con-trick that is. Taking a sweet little calf away from its mum, just so we can have milk in our tea. It's not fair is it?"

Gerry sensed he now had an audience: the cactus. "Even eating the accidental dead. I can raise less objection to someone who wants to eat my just-deceased flesh, although they might get a bit pissed if they did it just at this moment!" Gerry convulsed in laughter that left him coughing and spluttering as he reached for another drink.

"But yes, I can get that – eat me you bastard, I'm not worth a light anyway. Let the cows live!"

He sat silent for minutes before, "How can you deliberately go up to a perfectly healthy young beast and slaughter it? Bash it on the head with a brick? How can anyone do that?"

He paused again, "Don't half taste good though don't it, a nice bit of fillet steak. Yes my son, I could do with a plate of that right now, with plenty of chips, mushrooms and tomatoes. And, my good and kind sir please, if you don't mind, please do not forget the peas. I like a few peas on me plate I does."

Gerry poured another glass of whisky, slowly taking the head of the bottle to the rim of the glass before pouring it too quickly so it overfilled. He sat looking at the glass, burping quietly.

"That is, of course, apart from the better use for parts of my dead body. The transplant surgery. Do you know they can never find enough kidneys? I like a bit of kidney meself. Often had 'em for breakfast years ago. Not now, of course, don't get nothing done for me now. My dear old mum said I shouldn't get involved with women, and Mum," Gerry stood up, raising his glass to the air. "Mum, wherever you are. I just wanna say, I just want you to know that you were right. She was a bitch. No, she is a bitch." Gerry reached forward to pick up the cactus once again.

"You may cringe but there is nothing very new about being a cannibal. I could eat a slice of that bitch right now. I'd make it taste better than a fillet steak. Take it right of the cheeks of her fat arse." He swayed at the thought, the cactus spilling small stones all over the conservatory floor. "Now, look what you've done. The bitch would never forgive you for that. She'll have to bend down and pick 'em all up, and when she does I'll slice a thick juicy steak right of her bum!" Gerry swung his arm violently, spinning himself round until he fell to the floor. He stayed there, laughing softly.

"But she can't say anything now, can she, the bitch. She's off shagging somewhere or other. Piss off cow! I don't want you now anyway. Talk about second-hand goods. You, you bitch, you're ready for the antique shop." He slumped into a chair, bleary-eyes staring ahead, breathing deeply.

"It was done in this country, it really was love your neighbour in them days. Love 'em, certainly do, cooked slowly over a gentle fire! It wasn't just them primitive places that did that. We did that. Still do I wouldn't mind reckoning."

Gerry slowly pulled himself to his feet, reaching for the glass to gulp down more whisky. Wiping his hand across his mouth as he whispered, "Problem is that everything is now done too much. There's an excess, ain't there little plant. After all what are you doing here? You don't belong here do you? This is a cold country ain't it? You live in a hot place don't you? So, what are you doing here little plant freezing yur bollocks off so much that you have to wrap yourself up in that fluffy coat? I'll tell you why little plant and it's for one very simple reason, it's because you made someone a nice little profit. Nobody cared about you, you do realise that don't you? No, nobody cared a tinker's fart about you. You are just a plant. A silly hairy little plant who doesn't do very much. You just sit there, day after day. Why can't you do something? Well, of course, you do do something, don't you do something? Eh? Yes, you make a profit. Just like me you exist to make money for people. Then the silly bastards part with that cash to buy stuff that they do not need. Like effing Mansfield. What did he want to ponce about in a Porsche for? Talk about last bleedin chance saloon. Excuse me have you found my lost youth? Do you like the look of my penis extension? What a ponce!"

Gerry paused again, hitching up his trousers, pulling his belt another notch tighter. "I suppose he was satisfying a basic desire with that silly little car. It was a stupid machine. He couldn't get his wife and the week's shopping in the damn thing. Had to leave her behind!" Gerry convulsed in laughter.

"Suppose it did satisfy his basic desire for sex, not that he ever got any. Still he was trying to get there. Fast car, get some good food and keep nice and warm. What more do you need? How does a bleeding video recorder help with all that? Can you shag it, eat it or cuddle it? Course you can't. Try it boiled or fried, sitting on it to keep warm would result in electrocution or piles." Gerry paused again, standing, swaying slightly as he looked down at the small cactus plant.

"As for sex, all a video recorder can do is increase frustration, imagine the silly old bastards who sit there wanking themselves off, they are all screwed up." He paused, "or should that be unscrewed?"

"I don't care what people say," Gerry was shouting at the ceiling now, "I just want to do what I want to do for once in my life! It is a freedom that very few of us are allowed. As a kid you leave school full of joy, it is a time of escape, of hope but too soon you realise that you are facing a life of drudgery," He swung the whisky glass around the room, "And I've had it up to here with drudgery. When you're young you think you are lucky to find a job. Then you find all it's doing is giving some power junkie the chance to make a short-term profit for themselves. They don't care about anyone else, or the plants and animals who they have the pri-privilege to share this planet and they don't care a fig for their unborn kids. What about their grandchildren and great-grandchildren, eh? What about them?"

Gerry had tears in his eyes as he sank down into the chair.

Paul found him, four hours later, still sleeping, the cactus out of its pot, was now clinging to the front of his pullover as it rose and fell to the rhythm of his snores.

Would She Do?

Those few moments upon waking were always tinged with uncertainty for him, he was cold and as he pulled at the duvet it didn't move. Reaching to give it a tug he came upon warmth, rounded warm flesh that led gently down a slope to a valley. As his hand wallowed in the warmth, he remembered. But just to make sure he glanced up at the ceiling to confirm that it was actually his flat. The crack that looked like a monkey's profile was still there, above. It was his bed. A little shot of panic tingled down his spine. He pulled again at the duvet, slowly this time, just gaining enough to cover his cold bum.

Nice girl. Beautiful body. Bright, intelligent, bit critical at times but generally she was OK. Funny, he'd always gone for short girls in the past but she was his equal, may even be a little more, well it was the way she piled up her hair that made her look like that. Long legs. They started at the bottom and went right on up. He liked that. Always had short girls before. Tanya was short. His mother had always said that Tanya looked like a young boy. That had worried him for a while, because at the time he really did fancy her and part of her appeal had been that she was so small, so perfect. His mother had made him feel a bit like pervert after that, like he was some sort of paedophile. Then Penny, she'd got wider hips but was still short. And Sally, now what was he going to do about Sally? Gerry would get over it, but Sally? Why couldn't women just take it for what it was and enjoy, then forget?

They were all short thin women though. This one was not fat but she was a big girl. That obsession with small women had worried him so much that when he walked out on Penny he'd shacked up with Barbara for a while. Babs was a bit of a bike, but she came without any frills. Give her one, she would be happy. Decide to leave her out, she'd soon find someone to take over, and not have any regrets or recriminations. He'd liked Babs. A good sort of woman. Not that you'd want to take her out anywhere but she was all right. She may not have been tall, but she had size, no doubt about that. A big girl.

Shacked up for a while? Well, it had only been a week. He hadn't been able to take much more. She had been insatiable. All night long. He'd been with that bunch of Inspectors from Bramshill that week. Twenty-five young hopefuls from the Police Training College for an in-depth study into the behavioural causes of crime. Lectures, visits, discussion groups, all timetabled to the minute and then, after a full eight hours work wading through treacle with the dumb clucks, he had then gone back to Barbara's house.

First two days and nights he felt fine. He was fit and raring to go. It was great to have this great big bucket of sex just willing to oblige. All the time. By the end of that second night he had convinced himself he would wear her down. That eventually she would get tired or bored or just too damn sore. But no. She was not so much demanding as just expecting a continuous performance. Nothing was ever said. Somehow it just happened. He'd begun to feel like a cinema, a 24-hour cinema. One in which they entered, just after work, when the main feature was about to start. That over, and there were a considerable number of gripping moments during the performance of this epic full-length feature, there was time for an ice-cream or some popcorn. OK, they hadn't eaten ice cream but they had grazed. Just grabbed a drink or an odd snack before the B film began. This second performance didn't have the same magic or quality about it, partly because the leading man was not a class act. It was clear he was past his prime. Had shot his bolt, as the expression goes. Once that show was over there was another interlude, perhaps the lights went up, time for a visit to the loo, even to watch a few adverts while lazily grazing again. Then, excitement would mount as the main feature came round again.

This pattern would be repeated; each repetition taking perhaps four or five hours to complete before it was all started, all over again.

Three nights later the novelty had begun to fade. By the end of the first week he felt that novelty was not all that was showing signs of wear. He made his excuses, and rushed round to Gerry who had offered him a mattress until he'd found this flat.

He sighed. This place could tell a few tales. He'd been here a good while now. Had some enjoyable moments. He was just thinking that Louise was the first woman who had stayed all night when the duvet moved and she peered at him.

"Fine hotel this is."

He moved closer wrapping his body round hers. "Fancy a cup of tea?"

"Oh, yes please.'

When he came back to bed carrying two mugs of tea she was sitting up.

"What shall we do today?"

He was slightly taken aback by this. "I don't know, shouldn't you be getting home? Won't Justin be wondering where you are?"

"No, he thinks I went out on the piss with a girlfriend last night, he'll assume I stayed over. Anyway, he'll be playing football all day today, plenty of time for the mouse to play."

"Football, I thought he played rugby?"

"He does but they all always call it football. Don't ask me why."

"We could go for a walk, grab a bite to eat."

Then you can go home, he thought to himself.

"That sounds nice."

He felt her warm hand move across his stomach and put his tea on the floor beside the bed.

Justin Time

They walked slowly across the park; Louise nodded towards a rugby pitch in the distance just as a whistle blew.

"That's Justin's team playing."

'Does that imply that Justin will be there.'

'Yes, I told you he'd be playing today, in fact that's him, number five, do you want to meet him?'

Harry peered tentatively at the shape racing across the grass in pursuit of the ball. He looked big even from that distance.

'Only joking you daft bugger'.

He felt a curious twist in his gut. 'Thank god for that. I thought you were serious.'

'It is him, actually, I was just pulling your leg about meeting him. Anyway, while he's playing at being in the England rugby squad I can get some clean clothes.'

He wasn't sure why she needed clean clothes, but was eager to put some distance between him and Justin. 'Good idea, the farther I get away from here the better.'

'Come on then.' She pulled his hand, then let go and broke into a smooth run all the way back to his flat.

When he turned the corner into his road, she was sitting casually on the bonnet of her car.

'Tell me you are out of breath.'

'No, I'm not, come on gut-bucket let's go.'

Her house was entirely as he had expected. Large, probably Edwardian, a glossily-painted front door, shiny brass fittings, designer front garden. Justin obviously earned a penny or two and for a wild moment he wondered if they could just swap places. Justin might not notice for a day of two. Inside it was all bare floorboards and calico, a few carefully placed antiques, and large vases full of dried teasels and strangely shaped branches. In the living room lumps of driftwood lay in a lovingly restored fireplace, either side of which sat two square sofas, with a pine table at the centre with more dead foliage displayed in a large glass tube. The kitchen was by comparison a miracle of modern design, in metal and marble. Even her office had been carefully put together, the desk with its back to the window, all cool colours, and anglepoise lamps.

'Do you want to see the bedroom?'

He felt rather uneasy. He hoped she wasn't going to suggest anything weird like making love in their bed.

'In here.' She led the way into a darkened room. 'Lazy git, he never makes the bed.'

She moved forward grabbed the duvet, which was hanging over the end of the bed and shook it out several times before allowing it to settle gently into position. She pulled back the curtains and picked up a shirt and a pair of socks off the floor and tossed them into a wicker basket in one corner.

'He'll know you've been here if you do that.'

She sat on a small stool in front of a large pine dressing table. 'He'll just think I came home and went out again, silly.'

'Yes, I suppose he will.' He lent against the door frame. He didn't want to sit down in case he had to make a quick exit.

'Are you worried he might come back?' She gazed at him from the other side of the room.

'The thought had crossed my mind.'

'Don't worry. He wouldn't hit you, he'd hit me.'

'Well, then, I'd have to hit him, I suppose.'

'God, you're so old-fashioned. I love it. My knight in shining armour.' She stood up and moved to put her arms round him when the sound of a key in the front door reverberated down the hallway and up the stairs.

'Fuck.' Harry froze.

'Don't worry, let me handle it. He's probably just dashed back at half time for his Deep Heat. He always forgets it or he might have sent someone else to get it.'

She put her head round the door and peered down the stairs. 'Who's there?'

'Sorry Lou didn't mean to scare you, it's me, Dave.' A voice called back. 'Chuck us down the Deep Heat will you, Justin's thigh's playing up.'

'Righto, won't be a tick.'

She went to the small nightstand at one side of the bed and scrabbled around in the drawer. She waved a tube at him.

'Here you go, Dave. See you later.'

'Okay, bye Lou.'

'Got any tranquillisers in that drawer.' Harry whispered as the front door slammed.

'I'll just jump in the shower. Make yourself at home, won't be long.'

He sat nervously on the end of the bed and then shifted sideways as he caught sight of himself in the dressing table mirror. He stared at the blank wall until she appeared from the bathroom in bra and knickers rubbing her hair with a towel.

'I'll just sling some clothes on and we can go and get some lunch. Okay?'

He nodded. 'Yes, fine.' Nice lunch, wine, another walk around the park, kiss goodbye, wait till she turned to wave, quick jog home, telly, pint in the pub later, early night. Not a bad end to the weekend.

They found a small café off the beaten track, well away from any of Justin's haunts and sat inside away from the window. He had insisted. He began to relax as she ordered a second bottle of wine, and it wasn't until they got back to his flat, falling through the door together in fits of giggles, that he realised she was still there. But by then it didn't seem to matter and he was feeling rather randy. He could see her across the park later and then have an early night.

Nature Reserve

The car park entrance was arched with white painted wood standing bright in the fading sunlight. Dark clouds of trees edged the roughly laid ground as the Mercedes sports crunched to a halt. Mungo switched off the engine and lights and was suddenly aware of the blaring radio. He turned it down, slightly. Looking out of the car window he shuddered. It was a different world out in the country, away from the city. The drive had been good. He must get out more often. To drive his car fast. He passed everything, all the time. Nobody had a car as good, as fast. Nobody could beat Mungo. But this country was so bloody cold, so bloody damp and so bloody green. Everywhere was so bloody green. He turned up the radio. This car was good. Red and fast. He felt the part when he sat in his car. He was the part. Mungo was the man!

He looked at the clock. It was well past midnight. Where was Paul? Why had he wanted to meet in such a god-forsaken hole at this time of night? Oh, so what, it didn't matter. Mungo would sort out Paul. That Paul was one shit that had it coming. This was a good place. What did they call it, a nature reserve? Hah, the stupid bloody English, with their animals and all their stupid green. Paul would pay for all this when he arrived. It was not right that he, Mungo, should be treated like this, not by this shit! He would kick him hard, kick him good, kick him in his stupid English balls. Keeping him waiting like this. When he owed him money. Yes, owed him money. Plenty of money as well. It was not good. Nobody should be allowed to owe Mungo money!

Across the park Paul sat hunched up against a wooden picnic table watching the Mercedes. The wind swirled through the leaves causing them to flutter like gossiping schoolgirls on a distant playground. He waited and watched. He could hear the traffic sweeping past on the main road, its dull roar reaching him in long waves of sound. It was cool but not cold enough to need a jacket over his black shirt and trousers. This was fun, he thought, as Mungo got out of the car and strode purposefully towards the toilet block shrouded by trees in one corner of the park. Paul waited.

Mungo was really mad, that sod Paul had kept him waiting too long. He leant back at the stall. A piss was good. Sometimes a piss was better than a fuck. Yes, you know, it is good. A good long piss. Worth the wait. It was good. He pushed out a little more, shook his cock, gave it a long stroke, put it away and turned to wash his hands. This place stinks and there is no soap. Where is that sod Paul. I gonna give him a good kicking when he arrives. Mungo bent forward in front of the sink. His hands stuck out, stubby fingers apart. He turned towards the hand-drier, hands stuck out in front of him like a Dalek.

Paul moved quickly as the lights in the toilet block suddenly went out. He sprinted across the gravel, which cracked noisily at the night air. Mungo was lying on the wet floor, legs buckled under his lifeless body. "Got you, you bastard." Paul hissed as he opened a steel door set in the wall. With the aid of a small torch he re-adjusted the wiring circuits and replaced the fuses. Paul grinned as closing the service door he saw the bright new sign that said, 'Keep Out - Danger of Death'. "You wouldn't listen Mungo my old son and just look where it's got you. Fucking dead! Yes my son. You are bloody dead. For ever!"

As Paul reached down to pick up Mungo a car pulled into the car park. Paul heaved the small man over his shoulder. A sharp pain shot across his lower back. He staggered against the wall, swearing softly as the sound of a car crunched across the gravel. "Damn, it's like the Blackpool illuminations out there. What the hell is a car doing here at this time of night? In this bloody car park. Why couldn't people just stay at home? Watch TV. Oh fuck, my back hurts." He groaned as he fell backwards, pinning Mungo against the hand-drier. His feet slid away as he crashed to the floor. Mungo followed, grunting as his last breath was forced from his lungs. Paul crawled out from under the body, breathing hard,

"Oh my god, not now. The car, those people, coming for a pee. 'Come on Mungo, get yourself up on your feet." Paul muttered, then said it again, much louder, "C'mon you mother-fucker. Get up, get on your feet. You chose to get drunk. Now we got to get you home."

Paul was yelling, puffing and panting against the pain in his back as he hauled at Mungo. By the time he reached the door he had lodged the dead man across his hip. Quickly he flopped a dead arm over his shoulder,

"Back to the car, back to the car we go," he began to sing in a soft, swinging voice. He peered out of the open doorway, searching for the car that had just driven into the car park. He couldn't see anything, blind to the dark night outside the tunnel of light marking the path to the toilets. Cursing ever louder, he pulled at Mungo, his back stabbing bolts of intense pain as he moved.

Together the living and the dead moved down the path. The lights putting them on a stage. The only audience the occupants of that unseen car. He lugged and puffed, peered and squinted into the gloom. Coming to the end of the path Paul stopped to recover enough breath and strength to move the few yards towards Mungo's car.

"Everything all right?" The voice was pitched high, sounding like a whine. Paul spun round. Mungo's feet dragging an arc on the stones. He could see no one. He turned again in the other direction. Still nothing.

"Over here." The voice sounded softer, practically seductive.

"Where are you? I can't see you," Paul shouted into the darkness.

Footsteps moved softly towards him across the grass,

"It's alright. It's only us. We saw you and heard you shouting. Do you need any help?"

Paul's eyes adjusted to the two slight figures walking slowly across the grass towards him. Bloody nine-bob notes. At a time like this. What the bloody hell were they doing here? Just as quickly he understood. The toilets. They were a meeting place for woolly woofters. Just his bloody luck. Always too poxy clever for their own good, arse bandits.

His voice was quiet. He hoped it was collected,

"My friend's had too much. Passed out in the toilet. Just need to get him home for a good sleep. No problem. Thank you. Thank you. Goodnight to you both."

He turned and walked dragging Mungo with him until they reached the Mercedes. Gratefully Paul dropped Mungo's limp body over the bonnet of the car. Looking back the two men had stood at the entrance to the toilets watching his progress. He stood up and waved,

"Goodnight. Goodnight and thank you."

Still they stood, watching. Paul supported Mungo and stared back at the pair. It seemed like minutes before one of the men moved, walking away into the toilet, and the other man followed.

Thank God, thought Paul as he fished through Mungo's pockets for the car keys. He found a soft leather pouch with the keys attached. As he fumbled with the keys, opened the door, then bundled in Mungo as time raced by. At any moment the two men could come out and see him, he just had to get away quickly. As he drove out of the car park Paul could see, in his mind, the two slightly-built men standing, watching him still.

Paul drove carefully but fast enough to keep in the flow of traffic. This was not a time to look conspicuous.

The crematorium gates stood black and high. He opened the padlock and swung the car down the long drive towards the square chimney poking into the black sky. He knew the alarm would be easy. The duplicate keys opened the main doors. He quickly walked down the passage to the electrical meter room. The key to the alarm panel was obligingly waiting on top of the box. Turning the key in the control lock produced a satisfying silence as the system stopped humming. The building was his.

Working quickly in the dark he pushed the loading trolley to the back doors. He flopped Mungo's body on to the trolley and pushed it through the double doors at the rear of the catafalque into the cremator room. The stainless doors of the twin chambers shone dully in the night light. The air was hot and heavy. The fans whirred into action in the next room as Paul pressed switches on the control panel. A duct panel twanged as the air moved into the great chambers. Paul positioned the trolley in front of the door.

"Damn" he said out loud. Mungo needed to be in a coffin or on something if Paul was going to be able to push him into the chamber. He paused for a moment, thinking, then rushed out to the car. Returning with the carpet from the boot he rolled it under Mungo's body. Satisfied Paul slowly turned the huge arm that opened the door to the cremator. The residual heat left in the chamber from the last cremation hit him solidly in the face. He stepped to one side out of the heat and wound down the door. There, in the chamber, were the burnt remains of a body! Quickly he closed the door.

He peered through the small observation hole in the door. He was right. There was a dusty skeletal shape in the chamber. The bloody cremator technician had left early, leaving a partly-burnt body to fend for itself overnight, knowing that all the combustible material would burn away leaving just the ash by the time the technician returned the next morning.

Paul roughly pushed away the trolley. It swung round clanging against the far wall. He opened the chamber again. This time with a long rake in his hands. Slowly he broke up the skeleton allowing the pieces to fall through holes in the floor of the upper chamber to the separate cavern below that acted as a collecting chamber. He recovered the trolley pushing it against the front of the cremator. It was too low, he couldn't push Mungo's body into the chamber from that position. Panic flashed over him, what could he do? Everything was going wrong!

He stopped, stock still, and took three very long deep breaths. He felt the hot sweat on his brow running in riverlets down his face. Fumbling in the dark he found a lever at the head of the trolley. He pumped at it furiously, grunting as the bed of the trolley slowly lifted until it was level with the base of the chamber. Mungo's arm fell off the edge. Sweating even more from the heat of the chamber Paul threw Mungo's arm back across the body. With all his strength he pushed the carpet and Mungo's body down the rollers of the trolley into the chamber.

As it came off the end of the trolley it lost momentum, teetering at the entrance, stopping in a crumpled heap of body and carpet across the entrance to the cremator chamber. Quickly Paul wound down the door. Mungo's arm again! He opened the door slightly and pushed the arm back inside with the end of the long rake. Quickly he closed the door.

He was in! Paul leant against the wall, the sweat now pouring down his whole body. He was shaking from head to toe. He stood quietly. Deep breaths. Relax, he told himself. Just let yourself relax. It's all OK. In a few moments he had recovered sufficiently to peer into the spy-hole. Flames were beginning to lick around the crumpled mass that had once been that bastard Mungo. The body was too close to the door so Paul was only able to see half of the lump but it was burning. Great.

Slowly he opened the door to the bottom chamber. The mixture of wood ash and pieces of bone that had once been a dearly departed were illuminated by the growing strength of the flames from the chamber above. What the hell was he going to do with this lot? Suddenly he remembered the technicians had pointed to a machine in the next room during his conducted tour of the crematorium. The cremulator. He went to look at it. More stainless steel with a door on the front. He opened the door. Inside was a large wooden bung. He took it out. A black hole. Time for the torch. He shone its weak light into the hole. Three large black tennis balls coated with a white powder.

It was a ball mill. Just a simple little old ball mill. Put in the bones and all the crap and the ball mill rolls around to crush up all the little old bits. No problem. He rushed back to the cremator. Mungo was now going great guns. Flames beginning to roar as they ate into the flesh. Quickly he scraped the remains of dearly departed into a stainless steel tray, obviously used as a transfer vessel and rushed them to the cremulator. Once they were safely inside Paul pushed the button. The machine rumbled into life. Wow! This was all working.

Good Morning

He woke with a start, sitting up, registering that it was pitch dark, turned and saw the shape of her shoulder in the dark and held his watch up to peer at the time. Three-thirty and she was still there. He didn't have the heart to wake her up, and moved carefully so as not to disturb her.

When he opened his eyes again the room was full of light, and he quickly scrunched them shut again, pain shooting through each eyeball. He had a pounding headache; he turned facing the alarm clock.

'Shit, I'm late.' His leap out of bed pulled the duvet away from her body and he stood for a moment admiring the sleek lines.

She stirred looking up at him. 'God, I feel like shit.'

'Me too. Look, I'm going to have a shower and then I must dash. Supposed to be at the nick at eight-thirty.'

'Don't worry about me.' She yawned and stretched. 'Is it all right if I have a shower?'

'Sure. Just pull the door to when you go.'

She waited until she heard the front door slam before moving across the bed to watch him walk up the road and disappear out of sight. She got up, pulled her shirt on, went into the living room and sat on the sofa. He hadn't even said goodbye. She made herself a cup of coffee, opening cupboards and examining the contents as she waited for the kettle to boil. She went back to the living room and picked up the phone.

It rang for several moments, before it was picked up at the other end, followed by silence and then a loud crash as the receiver was dropped. She heard Dee shout 'fuck' in the distance and listened to the noises as she scrabbled for the phone.

'Dee, it's Louise.'

'What the fuck is the time?'

'Sorry, it's early.'

'For god's sake, Lou. It's the middle of the bloody night.'

'I've got something to tell you.'

'What?'

Louise giggled nervously. 'I've really done it this time.'

'Don't tell me you've taken vows.' Dee snorted loudly down the phone.

'No, worse, I think I've left Justin.'

'What... where are you?'

'Well, that's the other thing...'

'Look, I can't do this on the phone, heavy weekend. Come round ASAP, but you'll have to take me as you find me.'

Taking Dee as you found her was always an interesting proposition. It could mean finding her in the process of chucking out the previous night's catch or just that her entire house looked like a bomb had hit it, clothes draped everywhere, the weekend papers strewn across the floor, overflowing ashtrays and the remnants of several takeaways half-eaten still in their foil containers laying about, cold and congealed. Or that she was having one of her frenetic cleaning bees, and was likely to spring the dust buster on you at any moment.

Disposal

As dawn approached he was nearing York. He turned off the main road and motored into the country before stopping under the lee of a wood. Having searched and removed everything from the car he carefully wiped the entire surface of the car's interior with a soft cloth. Everything was meticulously polished clean.

Satisfied with his work he walked purposely into the wood. Returning to the car he drove slowly towards the old city.

It was race day and as he reached the edge of the city a group of horse boxes travelling in convoy slowed his progress. He was grateful to slip in behind their procession. At the race course he pulled into a car park, paid at the gate, ignoring the cheerful shout of 'You're in good time' from the attendant. He took the Mercedes across the park to the fence close to the track. He sat in the car for an hour before locking all the doors, strolling across the racecourse through the gathering crowds before finding a cab to take him to the railway station where he caught a train to London.

The train was shabby, the great days of British Rail had gone. Here the surface gloss of designed hype was rapidly ruined by the public. It was not the dear old traveller in the railway carriage's fault, it was just that those luvvy types commissioned by privatised greed merchants had no real conception of needs or practicalities. It had looked good on paper, it had seemed cheap enough to the rail company's owners, so who cares. Paul bought a cup of coffee in a paper cup and a paper sandwich from a poor scruff who had dejectedly pushed a snacks trolley down the long carriage towards him without selling anything. Custom was not good that day, and the repetitive journey from Edinburgh to London had clearly lost its glamour for this man. Paul looked at the hunched middle-aged figure, saw his greasy hair, untidily slicked across the balding dome, the suit drooped over the diminishing frame, the cheap glasses that kept sliding down a bony nose. The man said nothing more than, "three pound seventy" as he passed over the cup and boxed sandwich with one hand and stuck out his other hand. Paul put the money in his outstretched hand, to which the man sniffed, turned on his heel and pushed at the handle of his stainless steel trolley with its load of cans, boxes of sandwiches, strange slabs of cake and packets of crisps, biscuits and chocolates.

As the trolley passed through the draughty carriage door by his side Paul shifted in his seat to watch the sad procession as it moved away into the next compartment. Door open, trolley through, door close, door open, trolley through, door. A life left the carriage, a life that knew where it was headed.

Suddenly he was aware that he still had the small bag with the items he had taken from Mungo's car in his jacket pocket. He pulled out the plastic bag, intent on checking the contents and then leaving it under the seat as he left the train. There was very little in the bag. A can of de-icer, a gold cigarette lighter, some small change and a soft cloth, together with the car key fob. The lighter was gold. He slid off the outer cover and carefully wiped all the surfaces with a clean handkerchief. He did the same with the can of de-icer, placing them both back into the plastic bag. He then paused.

Putting them back into the bag together was not a good idea, he would throw them out of the window, at intervals as the train journeyed to London. The gold lighter was expensive, and well engineered, and it troubled him to throw away such a beautiful item, but needs must. He then turned to the cloth. It was simply a piece of gauze, probably meant to clean the windscreen, although it looked as if it had never been used. He stuffed it into his pocket, it may come in useful, and was totally innocuous. He then turned to the key fob, and realised that it was not just oddments of leather with a key ring attached. It was a pouch. It was, in fact, quite large, fitting comfortably into the palm of his hand. It was made of beautifully soft black calfskin, its top pulled together with a leather lace, bound at each end with thin silver wire strands. The car key was clipped to the side of the pouch. He looked carefully at the whole arrangement. It was very well made. This was no ordinary car key fob. Carefully he pulled at the leather thong and opened the mouth of the pouch.

Inside was a shiny blob of white cloth. He took it out of the pouch. It was silk, creamy white silk, that slid across his outstretched palm. It too was held by a small thong, its leather a matching creamy white. Paul laid all the items out on the table before him. The coffee, sandwich box to the left, the plastic bag with the de-icer and cigarette lighter in front of him, the black and white pouches to his right. The train was picking up speed, making that swaying sensation from side to side that gives the comfort of safe, speedy travel by train. He picked up the white purse; he could feel it held something that had a hard, gritty feel. As the train shuddered softly down the track Paul slowly opened the delicate silk purse and found a number of small papers parcels. Opening one he poured out its contents on to the calfskin pouch.

A shower of diamonds spilled out on to the soft black leather, catching the lights as they fell, continuing to sparkle, reflecting the movement as the train sped along. Paul gasped involuntarily, then quickly looked around. There was no one else close to his end of the carriage. He peered closely at the stones. Some were big, very big for diamonds. Paul knew immediately these were no ordinary stones. Quickly he put them all back into the silk purse, then into the black pouch and tied the leather thong around its top as tight as he could. Glancing guiltily around the carriage once more he stuffed the pouch inside his jacket pocket, next to his heart.

He sat in quiet contemplation for a few moments. This was a big moment in his life. Here were choices to be made that could have profound, if not fatal, consequences. To throw any of it away was to risk it being found, by chance perhaps. To keep it was clearly dangerous. Any one of these items could link him to the car, then to Mungo, who had disappeared. So? A rotten vicious little crook had decided to move away. Why should that cause anyone a problem? He was not liked, by anyone. He was hated by most. No tears would be spilt over Mungo. He was yesterday. Paul could be tomorrow. This little lot could give him the start he deserved, get him out of the shit, once and for all.

He'd have to work it all out with some care. This was not a time for hasty decisions.

Shall I?

"Let me make sure I have got this right," said Dee, as she tucked herself into a big easy chair, "you have left Justin."

Louise nodded. "Well, sort of."

Dee's place looked tidy, for a change. The living room had Dee's big chair, a sofa bed, a coffee table and several beanbags. Beanbags for goodness sake, it was like living in a time warp. Dried flowers hung in bunches around the fireplace, there were even some Xmas cards hanging from a ribbon in the corner.

"What do you mean 'sort of', how can you sort of leave someone, either you have or you haven't?" Dee frowned.

"I met this man called Harry on the Internet and we met for coffee last week. We had a sort of date for Saturday night and one thing led to another and I've sort of moved in with him, although he doesn't know it yet."

Dee sat bolt up right forcing Louise off the chair. "Sort of moved in with a man you met on the Internet?"

Louise slid on to the floor and sat looking up at the horrified face of Dee looking down at her. "He's really nice."

"You've sort of moved in with a complete stranger you met on the Internet?"

"He's a policeman, a detective sergeant."

"Oh, that's all right then. For god's sake Louise what is the matter with you?"

Louise stood up. "I went to a party with him, I must admit it was a bit of an eye opener, but then I think that was a good thing, because I saw him warts and all within a very short time. I know exactly what I'm getting into, which is more than I can say for Justin."

Dee sat ramrod straight in her chair and watched Louise carefully negotiate her bottom into a beanbag.

"What do you mean?"

"Well, it was funny really, the party was a sort of celebration. His best mate was moving in with his girlfriend who just happened to be an ex of Harry's, in fact she left him for Gerry, that's the guy that's moving in with Sally, Harry's ex. He didn't want to go at first because both his ex-wives were going to be there, but I persuaded him. Anyway, things were going well until Sally got drunk and decided she still loved Harry, which was probably after she caught us at it in Aunt Maude's bed, and announced that she didn't want to move in with Gerry after all. Anyway, it was all Harry's fault for screwing her the week before. Tanya, his first wife, was furious, and the other one, I forget her name, is a drug addict so she was out of it most of the time. I was exhausted by the end of the evening."

"And I thought I was a bit free with my affections. Bloody hell, Louise."

"You'll have to meet him. He's lovely. He works at the local nick, specialises in drugs and stuff, he's a bit older than me but that doesn't matter, and he's got a nice little flat in Hornsey."

"Oh, well, what more could one ask for."

"Don't be horrible."

"Sorry but it all sounds a bit improbable. And you still haven't explained what sort of moving in with him means?"

"Well, I stayed the night with him on Saturday and then one thing led to another and I stayed Sunday. He thinks I'm going to be gone by the time he gets back from work tonight but I just can't face the thought of going home to Justin. I really think Harry might be the one."

"Oh for fucks sake Louise. Don't you think he's going to notice that you're still there?"

"Well, yes of course, but I thought he might get used to the idea if I hung around long enough."

"Great game plan, Lou." Dee leant forward to pick up a packet of cigarettes, took one out and lit it, exhaling a cloud of smoke. "Come on darling. Justin's not that bad. Plenty of money, good-looking and big. What more could a woman want?"

Louise shrugged, "I know, I know that's what it must have looked like but you don't know the truth. Justin was not what he seemed."

Dee laughed, "don't tell me his dongle wasn't up to it."

"No, it all works when it wants to. It's just that most of the time I end up feeling like a place for him to put it. Do you know what I mean? He wakes up in the morning with a hard-on and wants to do something with it. I'm supposed to be grateful."

"You should try the single life darling. They come in here desperate to please. Pleading for it. That's the way I like it."

"You're probably right. I know I just end up feeling used."

"Come here darling. Come and curl up in this big chair with me and tell me all about it."

Louise sat timidly on the edge of the seat. Dee pulled her back, wrapping her arms around her friend. Louise burst into tears.

"There sweetheart. Cry it out. It will do you the world of good."

Louise sobbed silently.

After a few minutes the two friends looked at each other. "I sometimes wish I fancied women," Louise wiped away her tears.

"Know what you mean but really, can you imagine doing that? Sorry, I don't think it's an option. You are lumbered with men my darling. I don't see women as part of your scene."

Both women leant back into the chair. They knew each other well enough not to need to talk. Louise suddenly felt very tired.

Coven

They were casting the circle; to represent eternity, infinity, spacelessness, timelessness, a totality of perfection. This was to be their protection, a powerful space radiating energy from the cosmos. Within the circle they could perform, with assistance of an all encompassing God.

The High Priestess, clothed in a long black cloak, moved silently forward, calling powerfully upon the four elements to protect her from hostile or negative energy. The air rang with her tones as they pierced the gloom. Air, fire, water and earth. She drew her sacred athame and consecrated the salt of the earth and the water, plunging the dagger deep into the silver chalice and earthenware bowl. Water she placed to the West, salt to the North. Facing East she reverently lit incense, representing air.

Moving clockwise she slowly formed the circumference of a circle,

"I call upon the Keepers of the Eastern Portal of the Universe to keep this circle and all who are within it safe from negative forces. O Raphael, Archangel of the East, I call upon you to aid us tonight for the good of all humanity."

She repeated the circle again, this time with a candle for fire, invoking Michael to the South. Again for the West with water calling down Gabriel and finally beseeching Auriel to guard the north and the salt of the earth,

"Hekos, hekos, este bebeloi. I hereby declare the circle open."

Paul shivered involuntarily feeling now contained within a glass dome,

"Thee I invoke the bornless One. Thee that didst create the Earth and the Heavens."

Paul looked around him whilst the High Priestess continued to chant before the altar. He could no longer see beyond the rim of the circle. All was black. The witches surrounded him, ghostly now, garbed in black. The Priestess knelt before the altar.

"O Maat of the divine Intelligence, you who are the daughter of Heru-Khuti, the self-begotten heir of eternity. Who stands for justice and fairness. Convince those that would judge me on this earthly plane to look upon me with the fairness taught by your unalterable law. Decide in my favour. Decide in the name of Amen Ra, lord of the law, who knows all truths. May this come to pass"

Her voice rose to a crescendo, reverberating through the circle, crackling the air. Paul lost all sense of time and of self.

* * *

He awoke in a bed, alone. Slowly the daytime brain reappeared but was hopeless at recall. These were not moments for thinking. Just let it all happen, let the force be with you. He smiled puzzled by the sounds from below. Someone was there, in a kitchen. A result from last night. Margaret was some woman.

The door opened and a tray appeared leading her beautiful blonde face. Impeccably wonderful. A vision from another world yet strangely familiar, "I want you to listen to me." Her voice was soft and warm yet full of strained desperation. My lovely, I am listening. He sat up in bed. These were strange times. He awakes in a strange place, in walks a lovely woman whose body he remembers with tingling pleasure, and tells him to listen. So he does. Just what do you want to say to me loveliness, talk to me from outside my dream. Tell me your troubles. For I can see you are wearied by problems that are not of your making. You are not of conflict. You are of tomorrow, my future. Talk to me, but first let me tell you something, important.

"Wait just a moment. I, too, have something I want to say. For some time now, before we met, I was considering ending my life. It had no meaning any longer. It meant nothing, to me or anyone else." It was a bald statement yet full of understanding. Shocked, he became aware that it was full of his own feelings. She was what he knew. Startled, his daytime brain woke up to the reality it saw before it.

Last night she had been the girl in the light at the witches coven. Margaret, the middle-aged blonde with the perfect teeth, from the crematorium. She had stood, smiling, confident, unapproachable but surrounded by a halo of soft light. To him it had seemed as if she, alone, was standing beneath a shaft of light from above. It had caught her hair beneath her cloak. She had caught his breath.

This morning that dream was standing, in a bedroom, having made him a breakfast of scrambled egg, toast and tea, and she wanted to talk. Well, talk away, my lovely, talk, for I will listen to my future.

Margaret stared out into the middle distance for some time, before turning to speak, very quietly. "I go to the coven to try and sort myself out. You will never know how difficult life has been over the past few years. The coven has given me support. Through them I have found the strength I needed to get through the next day. There is a power greater than ourselves. I am convinced of that, but the Christian church, the godly holy catholic apostolic church did not embrace me. It did not seem to have sufficient charm or sensibility to be relevant to my world. I see the priests of the churches every day, and they do not impress me. The coven can give me more than the church. That took time to understand. You know, you are brought up with all things bright and beautiful, and going to church for all the important bits of your life. Christenings, marriages, deaths, then they give you Christmas and Easter and, for me, loads of guilt. You go, not because you really believe that Christ was the son of God. You know he was a good guy but he was a rebel. There are plenty of blokes like him about, even today. These days they lose out more quickly because the media coverage is that much greater, and they can get shot more easily."

She paused and poured his tea. Smilingly she handed him the cup. He nodded thanks and sipped and crunched,

"So out goes the dear old establishment. Isn't that the problem with this country? I'm not sure that Wicca is the right way, but it has opened my eyes."

"Wicca?"

"It's a fairly new form of the craft, came to life when the Witchcraft Act was repealed years ago, in the 1950s I think."

He was not sure he knew where this was going. Last night had moved him, in many ways. He was not sure if he could handle the emotions welling up inside him. Where are we going, can I handle all this, he silently measured.

"I talked of wanting to end it all. Now you do give me a glimmer of hope. For some time now, standing behind me there has been a man, a man from a different world. Slowly he was trying to put his arms around me. I didn't understand what this meant, but I knew I must not resist, for it would all work out in the end."

"And that man is me?,"

"Do you think so? We shall see, perhaps you're right."

"Yea, Mister Right." He crunched at the last piece of toast, "So, we are thrown together by the clan. I thank the clan. They have taste and discernment. Where does that leave us now?"

"I don't rightly know. How was the scrambled egg?"

"For me it was OK."

She gently touched his arm, "Well that's all we have to worry about right now, isn't it? That's the right way to live your life. One second at a time. Because that's what your life is. It is the here and now. What's just happened has gone, and cannot be changed. We don't know what will happen, and probably can't change that much either."

Paul laughed, "I can tell you that none of the plans I've ever made have come to anything. Not one."

Margaret turned away, suddenly serious, head downcast. Paul lifted her chin, turning her head to gaze into her eyes.

"Are you going to be like all the rest?"

"How do you mean?"

"All my life men have treated me like some sort of bimbo. An object, to use, to possess, to parade before their friends. I'm not like that. There is more to me and you must accept that."

"Fine, I'll try and remember beautiful one but this beast will find it difficult to cope. I'm not sure why, put it down to single-sex schools and a distinct lack of self esteem. Good-looking intelligent women have not been part of my scene and handling that now will be a new experience."

They talked, and as they did so he kept looking at her, finding a way in. Gradually the brittle responses of their earlier meetings had softened as they came to understand each other a little more. They moved beyond the immediate attraction felt by the lonely.

There was often a chilling realism the morning after that destroyed the enthusiasm of the previous night. Yet now it all seemed so natural. Time was standing still and they had always been there, or here. Suddenly he felt like crying, tears began to stream down his face as he sobbed uncontrollably. Her arms held him close and together they wept. He felt the tensions of his life drain away. "You, you." For minutes they cried. Stopping only to cry, "You" or "I know, I know." There was nothing but the pleasure of crying.

They crouched on the bed, hugging each other. "Look out there," he said, "That's a bright new world, it's wonderful and it belongs to us. I'm full of pain right now. Not sure how I can get through what's happened, what I've done."

"Just don't think about it. Whatever has happened will pass. Time will heal. It will cover up all the wounds. Just allow the layers of your new life to gently cover up your past. There's no need to rationalise. Whatever you've done with your life so far was because that was the path chosen for you."

"It's been a bloody hard road so far." Paul grunted.

"Perhaps, but there were reasons why you had to take that journey. Sometimes a dramatic event is needed to turn your head away from the past. To help you look at the future."

"Are you saying that everything we do is pre-ordained?"

"It's not quite like that. We do have challenges, perhaps conflicts that have been left unresolved from a previous life. In this lifetime we must work through those."

"But I'm not sure that makes sense. Do we go from life to life?"

"Perhaps, some people believe that. The Buddhists, for example, although I think they spend too much time making amends for the mistakes they perceive they've made in previous lives. I'd rather take each day as it comes."

"You could end up doing penance all the time if you worried about the mistakes you've made, not just in this life, but in previous lives. I can't get my head round all that. For me life is energy. Energy can't be destroyed. It just changes from one state to another. That's what global warming is all about, burning stuff that's millions of years old where energy is stored. We release that energy, breaking it down to its constituent parts, and that includes pollutants. I get that. But to tell me that I come back, as another person. That's hard." He fell back onto the pillows on the bed.

She smiled, picking up both of his hands, holding him softly. "The energy is the key. We each have that ball of energy. I can't describe what it is, just like we don't really understand about magnetism, or life, death or how a seed breaks open to create new life. There are forms of energy we don't understand. Perhaps there are other parallel worlds, who knows?"

"OK, for now I'll just let it wash over me. Now, let's transfer some energy between us."

I'm Here

Louise let herself into the flat with the spare key she had earlier found hanging in the kitchen, she heard the phone ringing as she closed the door and ran up the stairs two at a time.

"Hello." She answered tentatively, wondering what she would say if it was Harry, but then realised he wouldn't bother calling his own house.

"Who's that?" The voice on the other end of the phone demanded.

"It's Louise, Harry's at work. Can I take a message?"

"Oh, I thought you might be the cleaning lady. It's Tanya."

"Yes, I recognised your voice, we met on Saturday." She was just about to say you're the one with gorgeous bum but changed her mind.

"How could I forget?"

"Do you want to leave a message for Harry?"

There was a small pause. "Are you living with him?"

"Well… I… yes, I am, I suppose I am actually."

"I see." The tone was clipped, taut. "Well, that puts a different light on things. We should talk."

"What about?"

"Harry of course."

"I can't discuss Harry with you."

"Oh, I think you can, in fact you owe it to yourself to find out as much as you can about him before it's too late."

"I think I know more than enough already."

"You don't know the half of it my dear, trust me."

"Look I'm sorry but I…"

"I'll come to you."

"No, don't."

The dialling tone reverberating in her ear was the only answer.

This Is Different

Paul sat in the park, watching young mums pushing buggies to the ducks, wondering where all this was taking him. Margaret had moved into his life. He was spending more time with her, at her place. She had transformed him. This woman, who he knew nothing about really, she had become his partner. From a casual contact with a woman who turned out to be a witch, to an invitation to an open meeting, where a circle had been cast, just to welcome and celebrate the elements, the changing season of the year, his whole life had been changed. Margaret had seemed like a dream that evening. Now he was loving every minute spent with her.

She was the most wonderful person he had ever met. Slowly he was picking up clues about her life as they talked. He now knew she'd been to a few places. She knew Paris, had sipped coffee at the Chatelet bistro looking over the Seine towards Notre Dame. She knew that the Pompidou Centre wouldn't let you take in suitcases, but that The Louvre would. They'd laughed about that, as she told the story of her strolling through Paris from Gare de Montparnasse to Gare du Nord, and wanting to dump her suitcase somewhere. All that was recent stuff, so she'd been in Paris fairly recently. To see an old friend. She'd said no more than that, and he'd not asked. She spoke some French, better than his, but that didn't make her a language teacher. She knew Cornwall, and Sussex, and Suffolk but probably no better than he knew Yorkshire, Cheshire or Devon. She was a mature, intelligent, well-read, widely-travelled lady. What more could be said?

Her accent was from southern England, probably, although he couldn't be certain.

Slowly he walked back to her house, through the park, down the hill to the Victorian terrace that sparkled with her attention.

"Hi Paul," she smiled, head round the kitchen door as he entered the hall, "had a good day?"

"Not really, I'm exhausted. I've been running away from a guy, but now he has disappeared completely. Gone without trace. And it's best that you don't know any more about all that." He slid an arm around her waist as they kissed. "He's gone and you have appeared. Both are very strange events for which I can find no logical answers. Everything I've done lately has been completely out of character."

She smiled. "Want a drink, a coffee or a cup of tea?"

He kissed her again, slowly, drawing her in close, then looking deep into her eyes. "It's probably not important, and so I'll only ask you once. If you don't want to tell me, that's OK, we'll leave it at that."

She nodded.

"It's just that whenever I step out of line, I get caught. That may sound strange to you, but it's true, and it could all go wrong again. It often does. I don't want to hurt you, nor do I want to be hurt by you. This is all getting too much for me."

She kissed him lightly, then ran her fingers along his lips. "I'm not going to hurt you that way. I promise."

He sighed. "This all sounds so silly, so melodramatic but I'm used to solving puzzles, and you remain an enigma. I want to know more about you. Who you are and where you've come from."

She kissed him again, he could just feel the pressure of her lips on his, and the soft sweep of her breath down his cheek. She cupped his face in her warm hands. "All in good time. When we are ready. For now I'm a woman who works in a crematorium, moving people from one life to another," she whispered.

"Until then I must make sure that I am the man from your different world."

"Come see what I've prepared for dinner," she laughed.

Tanya's Coming!

She put the phone down, suddenly gripped by fear. What had she done? Why had she told her she was living with him? She decided not to answer the door and then realised that Tanya would probably phone Harry anyway and demand an explanation. She would just have to brazen it out, pretend that it was true and hope to god that Harry didn't find out or that by the time he did, she would be living with him. She crossed her fingers, took a deep breath and ran frenetically around the flat tidying up. She jumped when the doorbell rang. Quickly pulled her hair into some semblance of order and took a deep breath before running down the stairs to open the front door.

"Hi," Tanya's voice was bright, her smile cheerful. "Look I'm sorry. Can I just say this before we do anything else." She paused, looking straight into Louise's eyes. "I gave the wrong impression on the phone. I am truly happy for you both, really. Harry has spent the last couple of months screwing anything that moved and it's nice to see him settling down at last. I'm still very fond of him, you need to know that. Not that I shall ever be a threat to you with him. It's not like that, not any more, but he is the father of my children and we did spend a long time together. The thing with Sally was rather unfortunate, but she always was a silly bitch as far as I was concerned. Do you understand."

Louise smiled nervously. "Coffee?"

"Yes, please." Tanya followed her up the stairs. "I just get so angry with Harry. He seems to lurch from one disaster area to the next. I was going to give him a good telling off, and took it out on you instead."

Louise motioned for Tanya to take a seat.

"I've got a good idea, let's not talk about anything to do with Harry. The less said the better."

As the morning slipped by it became clear they shared common interests. They talked about art, music and modern dance. Tanya worked as an artist, designing fabrics for a range of clients. Louise found she admired the other woman's tenacity. She lived in a harsh commercial world yet retained her sensitivity and a great sense of fun. Soon they were laughing at each other's stories and retelling their reactions to concerts and exhibitions they had both attended over the years.

Louise outlined the plot of her novel with Tanya immediately giving her several useful suggestions. Suddenly it was a constructive experience to talk through some of her problems without embarrassment. To share with someone who both understood and cared. When they got hungry she prepared a lunch using the food she had intended for the surprise supper. A simple salad, with fresh bread, olives and houmus, washed down with apple juice. Tanya talked of her women's groups, of the range of different activities in which she was involved.

Louise had almost forgotten that she didn't actually live in the flat, when she heard the sound of Harry's key in the door, his footsteps on the stairs. He paused in the doorway, his gaze taking in the women seated side by side on the sofa.

"Harry." Tanya smiled brightly at him.

"What the fuck is going on here?" His eyes moved to confront Louise.

Louise took the bull by the horns. "Nothing, we've had a wonderful afternoon chatting."

"I bet you have, and I can imagine who the subject of your conversation was." He put his briefcase down,

'"When shall we three meet again in thunder, lightning or in rain?"

"Oh, don't get all paranoid, we haven't talked about you at all, have we Louise?"' Tanya stood up. "Anyway, I must dash." She turned to Louise. "I'll give you a ring later in the week, we can have lunch."

"Lovely, I'll see you out."

Harry eyed them doubtfully. "Bye, Tanya."

"Bye, Harry."

When Louise came back upstairs, Harry was sitting on the sofa, a perplexed expression on his face. She took a deep breath.

"Sorry about that. I was going to get a meal ready for you. Sort of a thank you for the weekend, and then Tanya called and one thing led to another. She came over for coffee and we ended up eating the food I'd bought for this evening and then you came home…" She stopped, suddenly aware that he was staring at her.

"Why are you still here?"

"I told you, I wanted to surprise you. Thought you might appreciate someone else cooking for you after a hard day's work."

"I see." But he didn't.

"Are you cross?"

"No, just mildly concerned and slightly irritated."

"Well, you needn't be. We didn't talk about you honestly. We made a pact not to. We talked about her work, my book, her women's group, counselling, everything but you."

Harry frowned again. "I don't mean about Tanya, although I must admit I was surprised to find her here, especially as I hadn't expected to find you here either."

"Yes, sorry. I know it must have seemed a bit of a cheek." Louise smiled, nervously. "Anyway, I think she's all right really. I think she probably turns it on for you, she knows it irritates the hell out of you."

"So you did talk about me?"

"No, credit me with a little bit of insight."

"Look." He sat up, shaking his head. "I don't want to discuss Tanya with you. I'm just not sure what's going on here?"

"Nothing."

"Then why are you still here?" He looked around suddenly. "And what have you done to the flat?"

"Nothing." She followed his gaze. "What?"

"It smells different." He said for want of something better.

"Oh." Louise sniffed the air. "I can't smell anything."

"Have you even been home?"

She pulled a face. "No."

"Is there something I should know?"

Louise took a deep breath and blurted it out. "I told Tanya we were living together, and the truth is I was wondering if I could stay here for a few days."

"I need a drink. A bloody good long stiff drink." He stood up and emerged from the kitchen some moments later carrying two glasses and a bottle of whisky.

"Medicinal?"

"I was thinking more along the lines of an anaesthetic," Harry said laughing, suddenly.

"I know it's a lot to ask and you can say no if you want. But I'll go as soon as I find somewhere else, I promise."

"Is that all there is to this?" Harry sipped his whisky carefully pacing backwards and forwards across the small room. "I mean what happens if we find we really like each other?"

"We can play it by ear if you like," her heart skipped a beat, "see how it goes. If you think it's not working I'll go. No questions asked."

"This is completely and utterly insane. You know that, don't you?" She nodded, not daring to breathe in case he changed his mind. "We meet, we go to bed," he hesitated, "and then all of a sudden it seems like I have a house guest." He gulped back a great mouthful of whisky.

She had been looking intently at him, following his movements, raising her glass, sipping at the whisky.

"And?"

'Well, to tell the truth, I've been buggered about by too many women, and all their crap has left me with a shell of a life. I don't know if I'm capable of a decent relationship any longer. I liked being married, but it's too hard to start again."

She frowned. "I don't recall proposing to you."

"No, I know, I'm just saying, marriage brings so much more. I've said it all before but marriage means two incomes in one life. Loads of money put it into bricks and mortar, pensions and also you can have a good time. That includes kids and all that stuff. That was a good time for me. Then you lose it all. It bloody hurts."

"I'm only asking for a couple of days, Harry."

"No, you're not." He threw himself down on the sofa. He sunk more whisky and reached for the bottle again.

"Hold on, you'll be falling over if you carry on like this." She reached for the bottle and refilled her own glass.

They sat quietly, facing each other across the small coffee table. Neither spoke. Each reflecting upon the decisions they had just taken. Eventually he looked across at her.

"Are you sure you want to do this?" Harry's voice was grave.

Louise kept her head down, watching the liquid swirling round. "Yes, I think I am."

"Let's consider this carefully," he said "Two days ago I was alone and you were married to Justin. Now we are talking about you moving in here. That is a big step. I have to admit that it scares the shit out of me. This was not in my game plan. Twice caught, never again. That was the way it was going to be."

"If you don't want me here, I'll go." She frowned. Straight deep furrows across her brow.

"No, I just can't get my head round this."

Louise stood up. "'Look forget it. It was a bad idea, I'll just go." She picked up her coat and handbag and moved to the door. "I'll see you around."

"Is it over, that's all I need to know."

"Whether I move in with you or not, it's over with Justin. It was over the moment I met you. I realise that now. I just can't go back there. I don't want to have some sort of sordid affair with you, sneaking around to see you, that sort of thing. I just don't have anywhere else to go for the moment."

* * *

The next morning he helped Louise at her house. Justin had long left for work by the time they arrived. They loaded up her car and drove back to his flat. She had packed a large suitcase with essentials and unplugged the computer in the office, which was now safely ensconced on the back seat wrapped in a blanket. She had hastily scrawled a note on a pad and left it by the telephone in the hall. It was short and to the point, she was leaving him, had taken the computer, and she would ring him during the week, and as a parting gesture informed him that he should get a solicitor.

"Are you sure you need to do that, perhaps you should leave that bit out." Harry had said peering over her shoulder.

"No point. Once he reads this that will be the end anyway, no going back. He thinks I'm a freeloader as it is. I gave up my job a couple of weeks ago so I could concentrate on the book. But I still have some rights. We shared possessions, and a life. I can't just walk away from everything, can I?"

He pondered upon this comment until they pulled up outside the flat. "You mean you don't have an income?" The consequences suddenly dawning on him.

"Well, not as such. But once the separation goes through, I should get something. I must be entitled to something out of the house."

"I think it depends on your capital. I mean, if you didn't put anything into it you can't take anything out. If you had children it would be different. Trust me I know."

"He paid for everything. He put the deposit down and paid the mortgage. I just paid the household bills. You don't earn much as a cashier at the Halifax."

"A cashier? I thought you had a degree."

"I do but what I didn't know at the time was that a sociology degree doesn't exactly open doors. I joined the Halifax from university on their graduate scheme, but I don't seem to have made much of a mark. I've been with them for years but I always seem to get passed over when it comes to promotion. It's probably because I hate it so much and I'm not very accurate, I lose concentration and make mistakes sometimes. They don't approve of that."

"Well, you might have to reconsider. I don't have that much you know. I've paid the price for having two ex-wives. I had to start all over again, buy the flat and all that. I don't have huge amounts of savings."

"I have a bit of money put aside. I can pay my way in terms of food and stuff. I'm going to send the book off to a publisher soon. That's why I gave up my job to concentrate on my writing. But Justin always made it so difficult. He thought if I wasn't working I should keep house, you know dinner on the table when he got home, clothes washed and ironed. Most of the time I forgot. He made me sack our cleaning lady. So I haven't made much progress on the book front the last couple of weeks. But now I can."

"Yes." He responded weakly, "is that while I break my butt earning a living?"

"Don't look so worried it's going to be lovely. I can cook, and do the housework instead of paying rent."

"I thought that was why you left Justin in the first place."

"Yes, but this will be different. I won't mind doing it for you."

Friendship

"Hi Gerry. Had a good day?" Paul was in the kitchen, cutting up garlic and onions for an evening meal. Gerry paused, taking off his coat to hand it in the hall. "Yes, thanks, and you?"

"Well yes, I took the day off, thought I'd go for a walk, so I went to that nature reserve up over Cheshunt way, you know the one I mean?"

"Yes, I think so. I've never been in there myself, but I've driven past several times. How was it?"

Paul glanced up at Gerry, who was reaching into the fridge for two beers. "It was great. I took a pair of binoculars, saw some birds, now don't ask me to tell you what they were, but there was one sort-of yellowy with a red Mohican haircut."

"Ah that's a woodpecker. A lesser-spotted or greater-tufted or something."

"It's good to know that you're as much of an ornithologist as me. Yes, lots of birds, no people, just me, the flowers and the trees and a bit of sun."

"Wasn't sure you were coming in tonight. Not seeing Margaret?"

"No, we've decided not to go mad. We've both been alone for a long time, not used to having someone falling all over us, all the time." Paul grinned. "You have too much of a good thing. Besides, she's out at a meeting tonight."

"I'm envious, especially after what's just happened to me. Been thinking about it all so I've had a shit of a day. Life was not getting any better at the old firm. I always knew something was up, you get so you can smell a problem. I knew they were about to fold."

"Hey, you'd been there some time. How long?"

Gerry pulled at the ring-pull, poured beer into a glass and handed it to Paul. "It's been twenty years Paul. Man and boy. Now its gone belly-up I'll be up a gum-tree without a paddle."

"Not sure you'll need a paddle up a tree but I know what you mean."

Both men chuckled, sipping at their beers, as Paul toyed with the onions in the pan on the stove.

"It'll be OK Gerry. Sometimes a change can be as good as a rest."

"Trouble is Paul at our age the rest might go on for a long time. What'll I do now I've lost this job? I've never done anything else."

"Relax, take a holiday, think a little. This is a great opportunity for you. I had to work some stuff out today, that's why I went for the walk."

"Oh, why was that?"

"Lovely walk in the country but when I got back to the car it'd got two punctures. Both tyres on the nearside were flat as pancakes."

"Oh no, what did you do?"

"I knew that calling out a breakdown service would cost me an arm and a leg, so I decided to do it myself."

"What do you mean?"

"I jacked up the nearside of the car, took off both wheels, found a couple of logs beside the car park, put those under the wheel rims, lowered the jack, locked that back in the boot , left a note on the windscreen to say what had happened and called a taxi."

"Bet he was a bit put out when you wanted to put two car wheels in his cab?"

Paul laughed, "No, he was decent bloke. Took me straight to his garage workshop, where they repaired the punctures, while I had a cup of tea in their canteen and then another cabbie took me back. Magic!"

"You lucky bugger. I'd have been there for hours waiting for someone to recover me."

"But Gerry, I'm an engineer. I think it all out before I start. You are a paper-pusher, who just has to start at the top of the pile every morning and hope you get to the bottom before you can escape and go home."

"OK smart-arse. What are you engineering in that pan?"

"Here, good sir, we shall have chicken in a tomato sauce, served on penne, with parsley from the garden sprinkled over as a delicious garnish. Before that I've decided to use up some of that egg mayonnaise you bought from the supermarket for your sandwiches and add it the smoked salmon we had left in the fridge. They'll make a good starter with a bit of olive oil on them."

"I see, it's left-overs again is it. The chicken we had two days ago and the salmon's been in there for at least a week. Did you check its sell-by date?"

"Always ignore 'em mate. Food's edible until it starts to grow a grey overcoat. Sell-by dates are for wimps, the owners of supermarkets and, how can I utter the words, health and safety officers!"

Carrying their beers and trays of food into the living room they settled down in front of the TV to watch Arsenal play football.

"Look mate I've got a proposition to put to you. It ain't easy to explain, and I'd rather you didn't ask any questions, but I'd like you to take a little holiday."

Gerry glanced quickly across at Paul, who sat quietly, looking straight ahead. "Holiday? Why? Where?"

"OK, those are the last questions I'll answer. Let's start with where. I want you to go to Spain. I've got a contact who lives near Girona, just through the French border on the way down to Barcelona. I want you to go and see him. I need you to take some gear for him to look at."

"OK, that sounds good. I like the Costa Brava. It's a bit more up-market than the places down south. What's the gear? And why this person?"

"OK. This guy is an expert in his field. One of the best in the world I'm told. He's a man to be trusted. I want him to look at some stuff."

"Paul, you've said that. What stuff? What do you mean?"

"Gerry, this is all going to sound mad, but I want you to trust me. We can both do very well out of this, and we both deserve a break."

"Hey this is getting more complicated by the minute. I'll need a bit more than you are telling me. It's all too bizarre." Gerry turned down the TV, suddenly annoyed by the banal commentators.

"Look I've come by some valuable gear. Not sure you need the whole story, but can I just tell you that the person I got them from should not have had them. He was a crook. A real bastard. I've no idea where he got them from but I will say he probably didn't pay full price for them."

"Paul, you're still not making sense. What is this gear you're talking about?"

"Diamonds."

"Bloody hell. Do you really want to get me into this?"

"Perhaps not but I'm too close to it all, and I just don't know which way to turn. You're a really good mate, and I need you right now. If you don't want to get involved I'll understand but there's so much going on I need some advice, somebody to talk to."

"Right Paul, let's get sensible. You've got some stolen diamonds that you took from a bloke who probably stole them from someone else. Am I right?"

Paul nodded.

"And you want me to take them to a fence in Spain, who'll sell them for you?"

Paul nodded again.

"This bloke you got them from knows you. He'll come looking for his diamonds, won't he?"

Paul took a sip at his whisky, pausing before he said quietly, "No Gerry, he won't be around any more. He's dead."

"Dead. When did that happen?"

"Just before I found the diamonds in his car. It's OK, there's no danger in all this. Nobody saw me take the diamonds. The geezer that had them is now as dead as a doornail. He ain't gonna say anything to anyone."

"But you want me to go to Spain. Are the diamonds worth that sort of journey?"

"I dunno, but there's over 100 stones and some of 'em are big. Real big. I reckon it will be worth the trip."

"Bloody hell Paul. But you reckon these stones were nicked by the dead guy. What about the real owners?"

"I can't guarantee Gerry but this bloke dealt in cash. He dealt in drugs. I reckon he built up this little collection over the years, taking a stone at a time from various clients. This lot is not just from one hit. Know what I mean?"

"Let me take that lot in Paul. Pour us another drink – and look the second half is just starting. Let's see Spurs get thrashed."

Dead Ringer

Of course it was Winston! He had known the instant that George's slow voice had invaded his flat. Silly sod had killed himself. That was not a problem, bad rubbish, and all that, but he had chosen to kill himself shortly after being released from a police cell. To cap it all Harry had been the last person to talk to him. Properly that is. Winston had asked him how long he was likely to get, Harry had shrugged, saying it had to be at least five years.

The lazy young Custody Officer had stuck his head against the wicket in the cell door and was now insisting that Winston had been alive and kicking every time he had listened. That story could be checked with the CCTV, it was unwise to trust anyone these days.

Winston had finally been released, a lawyer had secured enough sureties so that bail could not be refused, so Winston had gone home, and some time after that his apartment block had caught fire. Luckily everyone had escaped, except Winston.

The police surgeon was finishing his examination as George said, "But Harry, there's something wrong. Sure the man is dead, no doubt about that. The body is burnt, most of the clothing is charred, or has been burnt away but I just have a feeling that he was not killed by the fire. Doc says his mouth and nasal passages look too clean for that. Says it looks like he was not breathing when the fire took hold of him. He looks as if he has been strangled. What I can't understand is why he wasn't found in time when the fire started, there was a lot of smoke. Just look at the place now."

"OK George, I'll get down there." Harry muttered.

The next few hours were spent in explanation and preparation of statements. After it had been photographed the body was taken to the hospital morgue. The Coroner's Officer was briefed sufficiently to let the pathologist and Coroner know what had happened.

After telling the story to his own Detective Inspector, Chief Inspector and the Superintendent Harry then had a practised version to present to the uniform mob and finally to the Press Office, who would handle the media.

Dead bodies that had just left police cells were not welcome publicity. Harry was careful not to mention that he was probably the last person to talk to Winston Dailey. So far, no one had spotted that there was no official record that anyone had spoken to the man before he had been released from police custody. Harry was convinced that would not always go unnoticed.

He would not be in charge of this murder investigation. They had already told him that.

In the canteen the television raced across the world, updating information on all the little forays media folk found interesting. A war here, a sex scandal there, a government foundering but usually dealing with all that which we find boring. At least you could rely upon the Beeb. Balanced, unbiased reporting of all the interesting disasters. Interesting and stimulating unless you happened to be there.

Enough, he went to his office.

"Hi Harry", Elroy always affected a mid-Atlantic accent. He stood, leaning against the wall. Long blue legs, embroidered suede jacket with a fur collar framing the inane smile on his lips.

"Get down to the Yard this morning with those prints. We need them checked out."

Elroy hesitated, "What prints Skip?" A smile playing on his lips.

Harry grinned inwardly, "The prints we took off that stiff."

Elroy's smirk cracked, "How do you suppose I take prints off a dead crisp?"

"You don't. I got the mortuary to cut off his hands. They are waiting there in a nice plastic bag, my big brother, for you to take to the Lab." Harry paused as he smiled up at Elroy. "Where a nice little man will do the business for you, OK?"

"Hey man, you've got be kidding, so how do I get them to the Lab. We got a spare car?"

"No sir. You get on the Tube. When a body has been burnt like that getting the prints is a specialised job. The Lab will peel back the black skin of that black man and find the pink juicy curves of his prints underneath. You got that man?"

"Jesus." Elroy sighed out of the door.

Tomkins stuck his face into the room,

"Got young Georgie in the Charge Room Skip."

Down in the Charge Room a gruff, burly Sergeant leant on the Charge Room desk. Arms spread-eagled, he seemed ready to engulf the small dishevelled little figure seated before him,

"Now look here George lad, it's time you stopped playing these games. Where's it going to get you, eh?"

"Dunno," the rough elf shuffled and sniffed.

"What am I going to do with you now. You've been nicking cars for days. Pinching one, driving it for a bit, then dumping it and nicking another. What do you think I should do with you?"

The sad, wan, little London face gazed up at him. Dirty blond hair falling over eyes, a bright yellow scarf tied round the neck pushing colour into the face,

"Dunno"

"While we're at it, where did you get the scarf?"

"It's mine, honest, I bought it. I didn't nick it."

"Oh yea, what with? Where did you get the money from to buy a scarf?"

His thin squeaky voice was sadly quiet, "It's true. It's mine. I bought it." The small figure slumped further into the bench.

Harry stood quietly, watching the young lad play out the farce. Juveniles were responsible for most of the crime on his patch, the sort that hurt ordinary people. Burglaries, petty vandalism, noisy yobs, shoplifting, stealing cars, they were all juvenile crimes. But what could anyone do? The law said they were sweet, innocent, misplaced individuals that could be helped. Harry thought they were little sods that needed a good belting to make them understand that they shouldn't do things like that again. Then, it could so easily have been him. The streets of London are tough when you are alone, with no one to fight your corner, nobody who cares. He came from those same streets as Georgie, but his mum had always been there, always she had seemed to know that he had been close to danger, about to get into trouble, and had stopped him. She was so full of love for him, it hurt.

"OK, that's the least of your problems. You nicked the Ford from Kentish Town and you are in the frame for nicking that car radio. Where did that come from?" The uniform sergeant continued, glancing a quick smile at Harry.

"Can't remember."

"Well, you had better start thinking about it sunshine."

"I think it was a red car up the motorway."

"Right sunshine, get in the bin for a bit while we wait for your social worker to turn up. Sit quiet, have a good think and we'll take a nice long statement from you when she arrives. OK."

The boy nodded as he padded obediently towards the detention room.

"I'll just have a quiet word in his ear, OK Skip," said Harry. It was not a question.

Harry had a way with kids, quiet, friendly but authoritative. He would have made someone a good dad. George worked the area, knew it like the back of his hand, knew everybody there was to know. Harry asked lots of questions, starting slowly, talking about George and his problems. It was easy, he cared about this kid, wanted to know what kept him going. Nobody ever talked to George. His mother shouted at him, her boyfriends tended to ignore him, his father was never about these days and social workers with wan smiles and positive caring attitudes came and went. Harry touched a rare thread mainly because he treated little Georgie like a real person, someone who really mattered. They talked, and talked, Harry had their suppers brought over from the canteen, fish fingers, chips and beans, with loads of bread and butter and sweet tea. Still they talked, about nothing in particular Georgie would say later, but Harry made a friend and got a lot of useful information that afternoon.

For a start George had told him about Mungo's car.

Go For A Drink

Harry had been stuck at the nick all day when he decided it was time to talk to Gerry. He wasn't sure of the reaction he was going to get but plunged in using his concern for his friend's welfare as the reason for the call.

"Gerry, it's Harry, how are you, mate?"

"I'm all right, thanks." The answer was stiff, unfriendly.

"Can we meet? I fancied a pint, thought you might like to chat?"

"Sally's kicked me out, and I've lost my job."

"Look, I'm sorry."

"She told me everything."

"Did she?" Harry hoped she hadn't.

"Yes, how she didn't really want to leave you, only did it because she thought it might make you sit up and beg. She didn't love me at all, she just used me to get at you."

"So, where does that leave us?"

"In the same boat."

"What do you mean?"

"We've both been fucked. That's what I mean. Bloody women, I fucking hate them."

"Right." Harry heaved a sigh of relief. "Well, how about that pint?"

"Okay, I'll be there at seven."

* * *

Harry spotted Gerry as he pushed the door of their local open and pushed through the crowd to the corner of the bar.

"I've got one in for you." Gerry pushed a pint glass across the bar towards Harry.

"Thanks." He took a long drink, replacing it carefully on the beer mat. "Have you seen Sally since Saturday?"

"No, have you?" Gerry stared piercingly at Harry.

"No, thank god, and I don't want to. I think we're both best out of that one."

"Yeah, here's to no more fucking women."

"I'll drink to that." Harry picked up his glass with one hand and put the other behind his back, mentally crossing his fingers.

Gerry finished off the last two inches of liquid and nodded at the barman for a refill. Harry drank quickly, pushing his empty glass away and picking up the full one.

"So what else is new?"

"I lost my bloody job. Years I gave that firm, and what did they do to me? Called me in to the office, there was a bloody woman from HR in there, and I spotted what was about to happen straightaway."

"Why's that?"

"Well, the loud-mouth tart is there, so I'm wondering why, she's not there to recruit me is she? I'm already there, ain't I. Then I spotted the box of bloody tissue handkerchiefs. Didn't need a genius after that. He's sitting there looking all supercilious, with this dopey cow beside him, legs crossed, flashing a bit of thigh my way as she tried to look sympathetic."

"So, what did you say?"

"Harry, you don't say a lot. Afterwards you kick yourself, knowing there was a lot that could have been said, but I just looked him in the eye and said, 'you'll get it one day, you bastard' and walked out."

They both pulled on their pints.

"Dopey cow comes running after me, saying I can go on a counselling course, and the firm will pay."

"What did you say to that?"

"Told her to stick it where the sun don't shine, and walked away. It's not fair Harry. All those years I gave those bastards. Counted for nothing. What's the world coming to, eh?"

"I dunno mate. It's all about money these days. Loyalty don't mean a thing. You're as good as your last result. It's not so very different in my mob."

"Except you don't get the push that easily. Ah, fuck 'em. I've got a few quid redundancy. No worries. No women. The world is my oyster."

"What do you fancy doing now?"

"Dunno, might take a short holiday. Paul's got an idea for me, and I might do that. Must wait and see."

"Paul? Who's he?"

"Bloke I met through work, years ago. Back in the days when I played the field a bit. Seems like a world away now, but for some reason we've kept in touch. He's always been a bit of a rebel, but we get along OK. I suppose we kept in touch because I was always in the same place, and when he came back from whatever job he'd been working on, I was there. We'd go out for a pint, have a chat, and then he'd be off again."

"What's he do?"

"Something in the building industry, an engineer, air-conditioning and all that. That's how we first met. He worked on our office projects, years ago."

Both men concentrated on their beer for a few moments.

"Paul's moved in with me. Funny really. He turned up one evening, all flustered, said he was in a bit of bother, someone was harassing him, and could he stay with me for a few days until it blew over."

'Right.'

"Well it's worked out rather well. We're like a couple of old failures really, I expect the neighbours will say I've gone gay, but it's really convenient. There's someone there, although he's been getting involved with some woman, although they don't seem to stay the night together that often, so he has a meal with me most evenings. What about you and that Louise?"

"What about it?"

"Tanya phoned me this morning, said you and her were living together. I told her not to talk bollocks but she said it was true."

"Well…" Harry searched desperately for the right words. "…Yes, she is staying with me, temporarily, I got myself into a bit of a tricky situation. I thought it was going to be short and sweet, but she sort of lumbered herself on me." He affected a hang dog expression. "Bloody women."

"Yeah, bloody women." Gerry laughed dismally, looking at Harry sympathetically. "How are you going to get rid of her then? Tanya says she had lunch with her round yours. Sounds like she's made herself comfortable then?"

Bloody Tanya. "I know mate, can you imagine it, I walk in after work and there they are, cosy as anything tucked up on the sofa together."

"Tanya says she was talking like you and her were set up indefinitely."

He was going to kill her. "No, mate, just a temporary aberration. I just don't want to hurt her. She's left her husband, nowhere else to go."

"Bloody women."

"Yeah, bloody women." Harry agreed.

"Perhaps I can help if you're that desperate."

"No, really, it's my problem, I'll sort it."

"You're my best mate, Harry, I want to help."

"I don't see what you can do, honestly, it's nice of you to offer and all that but I've got to do my own dirty work. Thanks anyway."

"No, no, the pleasure will be all mine."

Harry didn't like the steely look in Gerry's eyes as he plonked his empty glass down.

"No, really."

"I've got it, I'll tell her that you screwed Sally last week. That'll do it, won't it?"

Harry laughed lightly, feeling his collar constrict his neck; he pulled ineffectively at his tie.

"She won't fall for that one." Harry chuckled weakly.

"No, but I did, didn't I?"

"Gerry, Gerry." Harry shook his head, looking towards the door, calculating the distance.

"She told me everything, Harry." Gerry leaned menacingly towards him. His breath damp with beer.

"Did she? Well, I wouldn't believe everything she tells you, She's a bloody woman after all, remember."

Gerry's face crumpled. "Yeah, bloody women."

Harry heaved a sigh of relief. He didn't know; if he had known for sure he would have hit him, wouldn't he? Probably not, Harry decided. They were after all, mates.

"Want another?" he said.

Catalonia

The heat struck Gerry full in the face as he walked through the open door of the aircraft, down the steps and on to the tarmac. He realised that he'd hardly ever flown before. That was very unusual, everyone around him seemed to be jumping on a plane and trotting off all over the world. He'd gone to Jersey once and he did have a glider pilot licence after a brief solo flight when he'd been an Air Training Corps cadet at school, but not much else. He'd always preferred to go by car and ferry, and stay in England or Europe. He remembered a mad weekend in Edinburgh when Rebecca decided they should join a commune, well not join, but create a new community, of which she would have been the spiritual leader, or Gruppenfuhrer as Gerry recalled feeling at the time. And they'd spent a disastrous week in Wales, with the kids, when Marcus had tried to throw himself over the edge of Beaumaris Castle and the windscreen wipers of their small Ford had deceased. He'd tried to get them repaired but all the local garages reverted to their native Welsh, with a smirk on their faces, so he'd abandoned the idea of repair and Rebecca had operated the levers from under the dashboard, all week. Aah, what it was to be young and ignorant.

Girona airport was homely, small enough not to feel lost, even though everything looked strange. He followed a crowd of 18-30 holidaymakers across the tarmac, young lads jostling loudly with one lone fat girl waddling along behind. Through Customs, and he'd tried to look relaxed, supposing that smuggling diamonds was not really smiled upon, and there stood a darkly-bearded man holding a small card upon which was written 'Gerry'.

'Hola, que tal. Are you Gerry?" The thick Catalan accent said 'Jeeree' and Gerry nodded, grateful not to be stranded in this foreign land. The taxi driver, spoke no more English leaving Gerry time to adjust to the heat of the day, and look over this land. Quickly leaving the airport and town they turned onto a sharply twisting country lane that ran through cork oak trees. Gerry tried to show his appreciation of the countryside, waving out of the window and smiling, 'good' to the driver, who grunted 'Los Gavarres' and no more.

After a stimulating drive around hairpin bends they arrived at a small village, yellow stone houses grouped around the superior tower of a dominating church. The car stopped in the square, outside a tall, well-maintained house. Gerry was ushered inside the house to be met by Jaume, a slight man, with a thick dark beard just like the taxi driver except this beard spoke excellent English.

The ground floor had once provided stabling for cows, pigs and chickens who'd made good, if smelly, central heating. Old pack harness cobwebbed the walls. Rusted meat hooks barbed the ceiling. The dim warmth was musty yet comforting.

They climbed the stairs to a large central room whose arched tiled ceiling defied gravity. Plain wood-stained furniture, walls crude white, flies circling a lone central bulb. Gerry idly wondered why flies chose such a life style.

Pleasantries passed as cicadas chattered faintly over dogs and glasses of sweet wine, then black coffee smoothed with brandy. The house, the village, his journey there moved into a haze. He asked to wash and rest. Following the woman, Anna, up the curved staircase to a gaunt room he was soon standing beneath a shower as it spat alternates of hot and cold over his tired frame. He then collapsed over a large, creaking, yet so comfortable bed.

The birds woke him, chattering loudly. In the distance a dog barked, others followed. Life had begun outside the roughly whitewashed walls of his room. Stretching back he gazed out over the recently harvested cornfields to distant purple-tinged hills. Sounds of movement below prompted him to shower and go downstairs. Hot milky coffee, fresh rolls and tart apricot preserve. The dark solitude of the house quietened its occupants. Speech was sparse and soft. Thick stone walls barred entrance to light except through small shuttered windows. The growing heat of the day could only be sensed through these walls. Later it would bring lethargic contentment. Out through the confining glass bright sunlight gave deep shadows, dark and sharp as they caught the profiles of buildings. Anna left him with Jaume.

"Have you brought everything?" The question came quiet, hesitant.

"Yes, I think so. It took some time to collect it all together." Gerry's tone tried to match Jaume's. He was going to like this quiet, brooding man.

"That is good," a pause while he pulled slowly on his Ducados. A stream of strong dark blue smoke blowing across the room. "Perhaps now is the time for me to look."

"Certainly but first I must have your assurance."

"Yes, senyor, you may be sure that I will place a proper value on your property." He paused. "There is my reputation." Jaume's thick black head shook, tilting upwards at the last.

"You misunderstand me, although I am pleased to hear that you will value them correctly, I need to know more, much more. I know these stones are valuable. Something tells me I want the history of these stones.

Everything you can possibly tell me. Anything is important. Do you think you can help?"

Jaume smiled, his dark moustache rising at the edge, "Senyor Gerry, I can tell you everything you need to know about these stones. For me to look at a stone is as if God looks into the soul of a man. There is nothing they can hide from my eyes. Which mine they come from, even which part of the mine, when they were mined, everything. Senyor the mining industry is carefully controlled by, how do you say, a few men?"

"A cartel, a monopoly?"

"Si, si, a monopoly. Control it is very strict. We are not talking just of stones Senyor. We talk of power, real power. These little rocks are just the means to power."

Gerry stood, suddenly tense, Jaume looking at him carefully.

"Senyor I do not ask why you, or your friend, need this information."

Gerry undid the buckle of his thick leather belt, slipping it from his waist. Sliding open a small zip hidden inside the fold of the upper edge he slowly removed sixteen small paper parcels and laid them on the broad wooden table before the quiet Catalan.

Jaume reached behind to a cupboard and laid out on the table a corrugated section of thick white card and a small square of thick black felt. From a waistcoat pocket came a hand-lens and forceps.

Meticulously Jaume lined up the small parcels on the table before him. The last he held in his hands, its tightly creased upper fold facing him.

"Good," he murmured, "the light is now perfect."

The mid-morning sun shone directly through the balcony doors, now thrown open, bathing the table in light without a trace of shadow. Carefully unfolding the packet he gently poured its contents on to the black velvet. The cut diamonds burst into life, catching and reflectively magnifying the sun rays. Shining like miniature stars.

Jaume glanced quickly upwards, catching Gerry's eye before bending to his work. Rapidly he sorted the stones by eye. Grading them as they were placed, with infinite care, into the cardboard corrugations. Passing through all the packets in a matter of minutes. Then, lens scrunched to his eye, he looked and sorted, sorted and sorted again. He worked without a sound all morning.

Gerry sat quietly listening to the sounds of birds, dogs, people and the occasional car. At intervals Anna appeared, first with coffee, later with wine and richly juicy black olives.

Jaume worked on, noticing nothing but the glittering collection of stones on velvet and card that sat waiting his appraisal. As the process continued he took more time with each stone. Turning each stone carefully beneath his protruded black eye. Holding it for long moments before returning it to the card. Gerry noticed that patterns were established and even to his untrained eye it was obvious that Jaume was grading the stones.

Abruptly Jaume stopped. Leaning back on his chair he sighed. He leant forward again and wrapped the stones into 24 new envelopes. He then stood gazing out of the open doorway. Gerry waited patiently until Jaume turned to face him,

"There is something wrong. My soul wants to believe but my brain tells me it cannot be true," his face was taut, the low soft voice troubled.

"What do you mean, what's wrong." Gerry was sharp, strident.

"Forgive me my friend, but for the moment it is for me alone to consider. You must allow me the luxury of time. Then it will sort itself out in my mind. Just let me say one thing. You have given me the greatest problem of my life. No, no it is not your responsibility. It is mine. You did not, could not know," he stopped, smiling, "I suggest we go for a walk."

As they stepped out from the coolness of the house the heat hit them forcibly. The square was now full of people. Short, squat, creased men, casually well dressed. Beautifully soft leather jackets, an occasional black-shawled widow mingling with the younger women, all elegantly dressed. Vibrant colours with skirts bunched at mid calf. Long woollen coats thrown casually open to reveal taut breasts beneath silken blouses. Dark Hebraic eyes, full of menace and pride.

And children, everywhere children. Running, scampering, shouting with excitement as they played around their parents. Such clothes for children. Each was perfect, straight from a catalogue where cost was no object. Boys in Bermuda shorts hugging their slight bodies. The girls dazzling with colour and style. Some aped their mothers and stood, like art deco statuettes. Others swirled and ran, wide skirts fluffed with trimmed petticoats. One little girl was fit for a bridesmaid in an orgy of organza and taffeta, her long black hair enclosed in a tight lace sleeve, matching black lace gloves stretching over her slender pale arms.

Jaume's voice came loud and cheerful, "Aah I had forgotten. We are about to have a christening. The stages of life are important in a village like this. It is important not just for the family of this new child. This life is for all to share. All must show they accept it has arrived and will come to play a part in this village. For us life without the children is not life at all." He paused watching the gaiety turn to respect and formality as the crowd filed into the church standing dominant in the village.

"You English can never understand the importance of family. We love and need our children. They provide us with many things. Our security for the future. Not only as ourselves but as a people who will carry on our culture and tradition. When you have had your culture taken away you gain even more respect for it."

"They look rich," said Gerry, immediately regretting the remark.

"Some are, most are making a public show. When a Catalan invites you into his home you will know that you are not just a friend, not just a passing acquaintance, you have become a part of his family. Most social contact takes place on the streets, in the bars, in public places. That is why they dress so well. They are proud, and want to present a public face that looks good. It is not arrogance. These people are not stupid peasants. This country is rich. Yes you are right. We are rich. Sometimes we need a foreigner to tell us that which we find difficult to believe. Catalonia is rich and proud. The Catalans are not ignorant conquistadors. We were not allowed to go to the New World. The Castilians would never have been able to control us. We were made to stay here. These people are strong, they work and they have the love of God."

The grey-green leaves of the twin olive trees flanking the steps of the huge church rustled gently in a welcome breeze.

"I've always believed that the Church hampered the progress of many countries. All Catholic countries seem to have been ravaged and abused by a caring, catholic church." Gerry grunted.

Jaume cried, "But you are right my friend, but the love of God runs deeper than the affects of a few bloodthirsty and greedy priests. Did you look at those people? Did they look like Andalusians. No they did not. They are not like the people you call Spaniards. What is a Spaniard but a mixture of races? These are Catalans. They are very different. A separate people. A different breed. Another language. We are all mongrels. All are a rare mixture of the blood of many races that have passed through this land. Did you know that many Catalans died in Hitler's concentration camps?"

"No, I didn't," said Gerry, wondering where this conversation was leading.

"Yes and that stupid German was right. His henchmen thought these Catalans were Jewish, and he was right." Jaume threw back his head and laughed, his cries joining the joyful peals of the church bells marking the climax of the christening.

"What do you mean?" Gerry was puzzled.

"They are Jews, and they have a long Jewish history. They no longer carry the name of Jew but in nature and before God they are Jews." He paused, excitedly drawing breath before starting again,

"At one time, in the long history of this country, it was passed the law. It was decided that all the Jews should be thrown out. Persecution of the Jews is nothing new. They expect it, and living here in this wonderful land had given them intelligence. Many knew what was about to happen. That it was just a matter of time before they were thrown out. So, what do they do?"

"I don't know, what did they do?"

"The intelligent ones stopped going, all the time, openly to synagogue. They built secret places for their worship. They hid their faith from the public gaze. When the expulsions came many left. Their priests went away, but thousands of Jewish people they remain. Catalonia was the gateway of Spain to the rest of Europe. The Jews came this way. They were protected, hidden away. Not just by other Jews. We are a people of tolerance and besides why should anyone listen to such a people as the Castilianos?"

"What do you mean?"

"One of the Kings of Castile had a problem talking. He was also not very masculine, how do you say in English?

"I don't know. Was he very effeminate?"

"Yes that is it, effeminate. His Court, in order to keep in his favour, all copied him. That way he would not seem different. That is why Castilians cannot pronounce an 'H' and why they are not strong like Catalans, because of Le Rei homosexual."

"Is that true,"

"Certainly, why should I lie about such people? To return, we talk of the Jews. Gradually they become closer to the local people. They stop going to their religions. They marry the local people. But they never stop being Jewish. Now all Catalonia is Jewish!"

"The synagogues never returned?"

"No, the one and only holy apostolic church made sure that did not happen. The Church is a good business. It is a wise man who keeps out the, how do you say, competition. It is still the same today. The Catholic Church controls. The spiritus. The Jewish part of us, perhaps that gives us a tradition. Where do we get Salvador Dali, Pablo Casals – Oh, if you could hear the poetry of Josep Pla. We are still peasants, but what peasants we are, rich and fulfilled. Peasants that can chase a dollar as well as any man!" With a triumphant gesture Jaume slumped himself down on a low wall, beaming.

They both laughed. The massive church loomed up beside them, crumbling stucco, grey brown with age. Rough cobbled streets, little more than pathways, rutted and ill kempt. Dangerously crude bare electric cables hung from wobbly porcelain mounts on the sides of buildings. An old woman scrubbed laboriously at a jumble of clothes before the village well. Gerry rubbed his hand across his brow damp with sweat,

"OK, I begin to understand why you choose to live in this backwater. But for me it's a little difficult to understand after London."

Jaume sighed, "Gerry, Gerry it would take a lifetime to explain. You have lost the way of the world. You always want more. You must accept that there is enough. Hey, now the fun will start."

The congregation were streaming out of the church, a babble of noise and colour in whose midst a baby slept. Showers of sweets and coins fell on their heads chased by shouting, scurrying children.

"More tradition?" shouted Gerry as he ducked to avoid another shower and was knocked sideways by the rush of excited children.

"Yes, come, let's walk and enjoy the country."

They strolled through the village. Past balconies strewn with flowers, under arches painted blue against the devil. Then out and up. Up a twisted dirt road. Each turn opening up a new scene. Until, looking back, they could see the village standing on a knoll in the centre of a wide valley. Surrounded by wide hills covered with cork oak and pine and the impenetrable slopes of the maquis. Miles away, down the valley, stood another village its church spire standing proud above a cluster of red-tiled houses. The village, hills and valley all framed by the glorious purple splendour of the ermine-tipped Pyrenees in the far distance.

This was not Gerry's world. With money to earn, deadlines to meet. Noise, dirty, smelly, constant noise. His was a demanding world, with overwhelming, scheming, crafty little brats stealing from the corner shop. Kids growing up to rape, drugs and robbery. To leave shit on the living room floors of little old ladies, to carp, scrounge, criticise and selfishly disregard the world around them. Such unfortunates were not the kids of Jaume's imagination. They were monsters, bred by a wayward society. They had to be fought, every day of their rotten sordid lives, for their own good. Until they conformed or suffered. Gerry hoped they suffered. If they didn't there was no natural justice in the world. You had to have a morality whatever your surroundings.

The warmth enveloped both men as they laid back and rested. Soon Jaume was asleep. Gerry listened to the chattering of the insects all around them. A lizard darted across his leg. This place was untrue. The realities of life usually won in the end. Some men, like detritus, rise to the top until it breaks down into its constituent parts. He sighed, thinking of the woman he still wanted to love. Room 111 had arrived with the rats starting to chew. He must accept the trials and limitations of life and try to make it bearable. The spirit slows down to accept the status quo. The inevitable becomes acceptable. Who needs change? Who needs this?

Why not? He could live here but no, there was, within him, a tacit unwillingness to motivate change. All in his life must be accepted with a dreary weariness, what could he change? He was only able to respond, not initiate. Now he seemed just to be waiting for death to arrive, but not with any consciousness. What else could he do? He didn't spend time thinking his future. He woke up every day, moaning and groaning and got on with it. What else could he do? He couldn't live here. How would he make a living? What could he do? It would just be a dream.

His life had never been very adventurous. True, he had married Rebecca. At the time that had seemed very exciting. Her family were different from his own. More sophisticated, more urbane. That was understandable of course. They had money. With money you could do anything. It was not that Rebecca's family were really any different from his own. Her mother had been very sweet at times. Very kind, even gentle. No, the money made a difference. With cash people became different. Wanted different things. Take Sunday mornings. At home his parents had stayed in bed a little longer, perhaps half an hour more than during the week. Rebecca's rose at noon, sweeping down the stairs in satin robes for black coffee and croissants. His pair had fried fatty bacon and large mushrooms freshly picked from the fields.

Such memories bring a moment of reality. What is it all about? After that we sit back and live a monotonous drag awaiting a short-lived immortality. A few generations from now and who would be thinking about his parents? No-one. Who would remember him? No-one did now so how could he hope that he would remain in the mind of a body that had not yet been born. What was it all about? He remembered his grandparents. His mother's mother had been special. A tall, even autocratic woman, who had always been kind, insofar as she had never been unkind. Aloof and vaguely disinterested in the world until the last time he had seen her. She had ended up in a mental hospital, tied into a high-backed chair, in a ward that stank of urine and cabbage. Then she had wanted him. He recalled her eyes, her look that had seemed like the face of someone slipping down a slope. Fingertips dug in but failing to hold as she slipped away from life. He had walked away. Dismissing her from his mind. Later, he was pleased to hear of her death partly because it took away part of his guilt.

Gerry lifted his head. In the distance a flock of sheep trudged into another field to scavenge the remains of a crop. Their shepherd standing alone, slightly apart from the group of animals as if uncertain of his place.

He sighed, the Darwinian drive suggests huge leaps forward. How much further forward is the shepherd from the sheep? He stands and waits for them to get large enough to eat, so that he may survive. Is that progress? It is just a chemical game. There is a basic fault in the design. A child is helpless and incapable of understanding the social structures. So we enter a frustrating, tedious process of indoctrination so that the child becomes an acceptable member of our society. Doctrines, rules, procedures instead of the warmth of the womb. Is this the correct training course? Had he got it right with his kids? No way. They didn't want to know that he even existed. Like his grandmother before, he too was becoming an embarrassment. Nobody wants a problem. Particularly if it's a problem parent.

Or is some godly force acknowledging that they can never get it right but nevertheless that will not stop them trying. This country believes in God. Who says they are right or wrong? Perhaps there is no benevolence. It is a major error in believing in a caring deity. It is really power crazy, and like some computer game enjoys destruction. Zap, zap, zap again. You are dead. Let's move to a higher level. You may but you will never leave. Hotel California says it all. He watched the shepherd move off to the next field. What a life. From field to field, with only the sheep for company. Gerry wondered whether he could manage the job. The loneliness was attractive. Standing in the sun on your own. Making friends with the sheep that you are going to bring into the world, to feed, to tend, to castrate, to shear, to kill, to skin and to butcher. It would give time to think but thought demands action, action needs money, shepherds are poor, unable to take much action because they do not have any money.

Besides money, bigotry and power are the tools of success. Often it is only a lifetime but isn't that sufficient? Why should most of us have to suffer whilst a few appear to gain so enormously?

What of those assuming authority over our destiny? Like shepherds over their flocks. They exercised the same form of benevolence. All smiles whilst they waited with a blood-stained knife behind their backs. To kill, to destroy, to exploit.

Do the religious institutions truly believe their missions, or are they also consumed by the braggardly selfish? Here in Spain bigotry is plain to see. The priest sins daily whilst admonishing their flock, but what is their sin? Who is entitled to set the standards? What dream decides?

Can nature provide any clues?

Gerry remembered his childhood, often alone, sitting in the branches of a large oak tree.

Perhaps so, the greatest knowledge would probably be gained from plants. A tree is not an individual in the same way as we would regard a person as standing alone. Regard is an important word, it is meant to suggest common acceptance, not necessarily truth. A tree may live for centuries. During that time the average oak is constantly attacked by over 300 different species. Each of those, shorter-lived, species is fighting to find a niche, a space in the world in which to live out its own life. It needs food and has found the oak tree provides sufficient for its immediate needs. That is why it lives there.

The cicadas buzzed as sweat dripped silently from his face; this was a hot country that overwhelmed the senses.

The oak tries to defend itself against these marauders. It doesn't adopt the same defensive technique throughout the tree. One area may react differently to another. One area may appear to accept destruction, whilst another will fight vigorously against the same foe. Imagine also that the invaders are Darwinians. Over the centuries they will have adapted themselves to satisfy their needs. They may bear little resemblance to the creature that occupied that same slot in nature centuries before. Yet the oak tree stands, proudly, able to sufficiently resist the attacks to ensure its own survival over the years.

It does so by being flexible. It is not just a tree, but a far more complicated entity with perceptions beyond our imaginations. It has had to develop along pathways that we failed to discover, or disregarded as irrelevant to our own fight for survival.

The tree is flexible. Man is intransigent, too single-minded. The tree shows that you can live, and let live. Move with the ebb and flow of the demands of others.'

Gerry broke from his morbid reverie, a small child stood before him, smiling and pointing, "Anem, Senyor, cap al la caçadors, ara mateix."

Jaume woke quickly, laughing as he spoke rapidly to the child, who scampered away,

"The hunters they have killed a wild boar, shall we go and see?"

Gerry followed across the square. In one corner a crowd had gathered, all chattering loudly in front of a shop front. Looking through the crowd he could see a large, hairy, black pig lying on a table. Dark moustaches wielding long knives chattered at the dead creature.

"They are describing the kill. Feran shot the, how you say eh, pig. It is the first one he has ever shot. Nobody in his family has ever killed a pig before. He is very proud. He is telling how it happened. I do not think it is really much of a story. They go to the hills in a large group. If you are lucky the pig comes your way and you shoot, and it drops down dead. You hope! If you do not get it right this animal is very fierce, you know, it can kill."

Jaume pointed to the rear of the room,

"Ah, see there is more."

Gerry saw seven little wild boar, like fat puppies, laid out like their mother, but on the floor,

"But why kill the little ones. They are not dangerous."

"Understand, Gerry, if the mother is dead the little ones must die also. They cannot live without their mother. Now we are to have a celebration, you will stay?"

They watched the men prepare a great pot of alioli. Cloves of garlic pounded in a mortar with green olive oil and a little salt. Other carved huge hunks of bread and toasted them before a blazing log fire. All the time the group chattered. The old man, grey waistcoat and gnarled hands, called Feran, was clearly the hero of the hour.

"We will have this food now. The meat must be inspected before it can be eaten and, anyway, it will taste better in a few days. But now they are hungry. The alioli and a little wine will be good. Now they cut up the pig. Feran will get the best parts, it is his honour. Everyone will get some. You will take some back to Londres."

They ate the deliciously biting garlic spread thickly on toast soaked in tomato, sprinkled with oil and salt and sipped cool wine while watching the men cut up the flesh. Slowly Gerry lost his initial disgust at the scene. Clearly it was stupid in some ways. Jaume had complained that there were no longer enough wild boar in the hills to provide sport. Yet they had just killed seven youngsters, their sport for tomorrow. Gerry was not even sure that Jaume understood. The death bought community. These people were together. They knew and understood each other, loved each other, cared for each other.

* * *

The next day Jaume said, "I am ready."

They moved to the verandah. Anna brought coffee. They sat and looked over the square.

"Senyor Gerry, amongst this collection are some diamonds I never hoped to see. It was like a dream, you know. They are from the Ramulkolta mines in India. Deep pits in the sandstone. The old miners used iron rods, crooked at one end to pull up the gravels from veins in the rocks. These were the lost mines of India once called the Raolconda mines. From this area of India have come some of the finest diamonds ever. 'Diamonds with a green crust which when cut are white and of a very beautiful water', so said Tavernier when he visited these mines many times between 1630 and 1668. We are talking of the great diamonds of history, the Koh-i-Nur, the Regent, the Great Mogul and the Tavernier Blue."

Jaume fell silent and sat looking out of the window, Gerry asked,

"How can you tell all this?"

Jaume smiled,

"Gerry we are in the history of diamonds. One of these stones is point cut, we gave that up centuries ago, others are rose cut just like the Koh-i-Nur and the Great Mogul. They are not flawless but most are VVS or VS, which is very fine. The culets are often damaged but they are only paper marks and they show that these stones, you know, these stones they have been around. They have been cut in the old style. They are not spread to make them look larger than they really are."

"How much are they worth?"

Jaume laughed,

"Gerry why must you always spoil pleasure with talk of money? These stones, they have the weight. Some weigh 3 or 4 carats. Weight is important in a diamond. Just like some men like the women, eh, the bigger the better. But the diamond should be flawless. You know there must be nothing inside or outside the stone but diamond. These are not so perfect, but they are very good."

Jaume paused, taking a small sip of wine as he leant back in his chair.

"What sells these diamonds is the colour."

"What do you mean colour. Do diamonds have colour?" asked Gerry.

"Yes of course, but how to describe. That is very difficult. How do you measure the colour of a diamond? You tell me it is blue, it is white, what does that mean? We have fashions all the time. They try and change the colour. Oh, one man will say, my yellow stones are perfect. No, no try these green and white stones they really sparkle."

"So what are these stones?"

"These stones are white. White. There is no colour. That is the way every diamond dealer wants to see his diamonds. These are premium stones. There is a magic about owning stones like these. They come with perfection, with history and with 'magic'."

Jaume hissed out the word 'magic'.

"These are diamonds for all time. They are better than gold, better than any currency. They will always hold their price, but you can only look after them, they will never become yours."

That afternoon Gerry flew back to London, a slice of wild boar in his pocket.

What Now?

"So what did he say?"

"It's a dreamy place Paul. Do you know I have a feeling that I should go there, live there."

Paul chuckled, 'Hey man that Spain has really got into you. Are you listening man, do you hear what I ask? What did the nice man say about the little chips?"

"Paul those chips, as you put them, are very special. I don't know where you got them from, and I'm not that sure I really want to know, but they are dynamite."

"What do you mean? They're hot?" Paul shuffled uneasily in his chair.

"I don't know about that and Jaume never said anything about their recent history. He's a diamond man, an expert in the nature and structure of diamonds. He's not a jewel thief or a copper. He was just telling me about the stones. How did you get to know him anyway?"

"That doesn't matter now, it was through the friend of a friend. I know a lot of people, and one of them knew something about good jewellery. I wanted someone discreet, so some guy living in the backlands of Spain seemed like a good idea. Especially as nobody would ever suspect you of much, and he only knows you as Gerry, probably would never understand that you were really Jeremiah. What were your parents on?"

It was Gerry's turn to look uneasy. "That's a long story, it's all about a relative. The stones, you want to know about the stones. All you really want to know is that the larger stones come from an Indian mine, and have an excellent pedigree. They are from the same mine as some of the most famous diamonds in the world. They are very good white stones."

"Gerry, don't take this the wrong way, but I do need to know the answer to one question. I know that my asking it will fill you with suspicion but all of that is my problem, not yours. I'll not involve you in any of this. We are mates. You've done me a great favour getting involved at all and I'm not going to get you any deeper into all this." He paused, taking a long slow drink, staring ahead, not glancing at Gerry. "What I've done, how I got hold of these stones is my business. I've got a clear conscience. Sometimes the world needs a dustman to clear out the rubbish. That's the way the world is."

"OK Paul. I want to know, but I won't ask. I've got the picture. We've been friends for a long time. Go on, ask the question."

"Well I want to know if he said anything about how stones like these can be identified?"

"He said they were old, he could tell by the way in which they had been cut. If that's what you mean?"

"No, but famous stones we know about. You know the stuff they put in the Queen's crown, they've all got names and that, so what about these, do they have any identification marks? Are they named stones?"

"He didn't mention anything like that. No, he said they were lovely stones, that most had probably come from India, and a few of the best had obviously come from the same mine. These are a great collection, but they are not connected to each other. Although some come from the same mine that's just because they are good stones, and this mine is a source of good stones."

"So they are not identifiable individually?" Paul took another sip of beer, slipping back into the chair.

"Not that Jaume said. As a collection, if they are a collection, then whoever they belong to would probably be able to identify the group. The sixteen packets they were wrapped in showed they had been grouped together. Each packet had a particular type of stones. Whoever did that knew his diamonds. They were collectors of rare stones."

"That's fine Gerry. That's made the whole trip worthwhile and my mind is now a lot easier. I'm going to tell you a little about something about my part in their story. OK."

Gerry looked straight into Paul's eyes, "If that's what you want to do. Just know Paul that whatever you tell me will be kept strictly between us. Nobody else will ever know. What I do know is that you couldn't afford to buy these stones. They are worth real money."

Paul laughed softly, "The guy I got these from had more money than he deserved. Now I see why he had them. They were his insurance policy, his retirement pension, giving him a ready source of cash whenever he needed it, they were easy to hide, easy to move about, and anonymous. And this guy needed to keep everything he did very quiet."

Gerry slapped his hands, "I've got him. He was a dealer. Am I right?"

"You are old son. He was my main supplier of Lebanese gold. Good stuff, and he knew it. Always charged top dollar, but it was worth it."

"He was?"

Paul's eyes turned away, the blank stare returning. "Yes, he's not with us any more. He met with an accident. I happened to be close by. Found these in his car. Took my chance and here we are."

"What sort of accident?"

"One that he didn't get through. He's no longer with us."

"Did you arrange that?"

"Course not. The thing is I took the chance, and we've come up trumps. He didn't deserve to have all this gear anyway. He was low-life. What happened to him was what was going to happen to him sometime. These guys don't draw the old-age pension."

"Paul, OK, I've heard enough to understand and I don't want to ask about the detail. You now have a valuable collection there. You can sell the stones one by one. Nobody will ever be the wiser. You've now got the pension fund."

"And you my son. I'm not going to let you walk away now. You deserve a share, and besides, being strictly practical, if you take some of the profit from my little deal there's going to be less chance that you'll ever shop me. That's true ain't it?"

"Now hold on, I'm going to stop and think before I answer that. How about another drink?"

Both men smiled, got up and walked over to the table where bottles of drink had been put, ready for an evening session.

My Son

Harry was grateful the flat was empty when he got back from work. He wondered for a brief moment where Louise was and wondered if she was out flat hunting. Stripping off his clothes he ran a shower, enjoying the hot stabbing stream on his face. He felt very tired. He shaved, cleaned his teeth vigorously then put on some fresh clothes. After a large cup of coffee and great lumps of bread and cheese he began to feel better.

He had planned to prepare some work, perhaps to work on a series of articles he was preparing for a police magazine. Instead he switched on the television, he needed time to think. There was something not quite right. Winston was dead. Mungo's car had turned up in York, and at the racecourse. What was he doing up there? Mungo was a city guy, never left London. He was the king in his little patch. What had he and Winston been up to? The European football competition ensured there was always something mindless to watch. Either the football matches themselves or the peculiar selection of pundits that were encouraged to voice their opinions. Football was not his scene. Anything to do with balls, unless they were his own, left him cold. Football was all about money and brainless devotion. Tennis was a circus with the same players revolving round the world. All that seemed to change was the colour of the tennis court. Golf annoyed him. It wasted so much time. Grown men hitting a little white ball with a bent stick until it fell in a hole. Well, I never. There it is. The little white ball is in the hole. Let's move on and do that all over again, shall we?

It looked as if England were about to lose the match. Again. He tried to imagine all the men in England gathered together in one place, cheering on their team. 'Jerusalem' he muttered. 'England's green and pleasant land.'

Justin sprang to mind. No doubt he would be watching the game. Probably be with the rest of his team, all dressed in England football shirts, shouting across a bar, slapping each other on the back. The male in a group was a strange beast. A huge energy took over. The individuals became part of the crowd. It was easy to imagine such a horde rushing forward upon an enemy in war. Beckham dropped a lovely cross right on to Rooney's toe. He shot! The keeper flung himself sideways tipping the ball over the bar. How did he manage that? If he could find Mungo a lot of questions could be answered.

Justin and Louise. Now that was not an item any longer. There was to be no Justin and Louise. Justin was on his own, and Louise? She was with Harry. Is that right. Louise and Harry. They lived together now. What in that small flat of his? Well, yes. They seem to manage OK. Place always looks good although there is a strange new smell when you walk in there. Harry sniffed, 'what was that smell?' He must remember to ask her again, when she got back.

The game rambled on. Portugal now had a two-goal lead and were tightening down, keeping possession of the ball in the centre of the field. The pundits droned.

So what's she like? He imagined the exchange between himself and his mother. What does she do for a living? Well, nothing. Nothing? Well, she is writing a novel. We can all do that young man, his mother would say, but is she making any contribution to the household? It'll be all right, he would assure his mother, who had always acted the matriarch version of Attila, the Hun. I don't understand you, mum would say, you seem to muck up everything. I'll admit I didn't like that Tanya, far too flighty for you but I have to say she did a good job with the children. They are both marvellous. A credit to you both. He made a note to email them both. Tanya had made some mention of a new job. Yes mother. Which one had the new job? He couldn't remember, was it Marcus or Sophie? He jumped to his feet as the Portuguese made another fierce attack on the English goal. The ball was flying around everywhere. Harry was convinced they would concede a penalty.

So what's she like? A sexy woman, that was true. A positive woman, with a soft mouth that yielded so wonderfully. An understanding woman, bloody well needed to be with all that had happened over the last few days and he just loved running his hand over her buttocks. Not that it had been his fault. The party with Sally and all that and Penny. And now she looked like getting a bit too friendly with Tanya. Dodgy that. Tanya knew him too well and they went back a long way and perhaps one day. But no, there was no going back. She had made her bed. He had got her out of his skin, at last. He didn't need her any more. She was a different person now besides she had decided to live with the ace dike Candida. If anyone was ever misnamed it was her. An archetypal lesbian. Big and butch and peculiarly stupid. He could never understand why his Tanya should get involved with someone like that, male or female.

He paused in thought. Perhaps he should talk to Georgie again, or maybe forensic would come up with something. Portugal had just scored another goal, right on half-time. Bloody hell! About time they used a few English players in the League. How were we supposed to win anything when British football was played by a bunch of foreigners. His mouth was dry. He made himself a jug of orange squash and a big jam sandwich.

Not been that way when he was with Penny, he had to admit. Then Penny and him had a strange sort of marriage. No sex to talk about. That wasn't strictly true, as Penny loved to play around but held off at penetration. She liked all the fuss beforehand but not the act itself. He had never worked out why he had married her or she him. They liked each other; they never actually had a row but finally just drifted apart. He had never come to turns with her pot smoking. Letting your brain swan off on its own seemed pointless. He liked to remain in control. Penny floated through her life. Not hurting anyone, making lots of friends. She seemed to know everybody and they all liked her but life was empty with her. Parties, feckless shopping, a round of pleasure but no more. There was nothing else to Penny. She was just nice.

Louise was different. For the first time in his life he felt part of a relationship. She was part of his life. Already he was used to living with her. Opening the door to his flat every evening was a pleasure. Every day she would have some news or have made some small change to the place. It was turning into a home. How did women do that? Within moments they could tidy up, place a vase here, move a picture, drape a curtain and all would be transformed.

The second half was about to start when the telephone rang. Harry looked at the handset wondering whether to answer. He really wanted to watch the next half uninterrupted with nothing more than his own thoughts.

"Hello."

"Harry."

"Yes."

"Where have you been? I've been trying to get hold of you for ages!"

"I've been here. Why?"

"No you haven't I have been ringing for the past three hours."

"Sorry Louise. I went for a drink after work."

"Right, don't let's worry about all that now. This is far more important. Get down here straightaway."

"Where are you Louise?"

"Kentish Town nick. Come down here as soon as you can see if you can do better than me. The Fuzz are not being very helpful."

"What are you doing at the police station for god's sake?"

"Harry! Let me tell you this is not of my making. I don't want to be here. This really is not my problem but I came because the police phoned me. They phoned you really but I answered worse luck. They wanted me, well someone, down here."

"This is not making any sense Louise. Why are you at the nick?"

"Your son has been arrested. That's why. You remember him? Marcus. Now are you coming down here or not?

"What for, I mean why has he been arrested? What for?"

"He's a drug pusher. So the nice sergeant here tells me. Now, get down here."

* * *

He'd not known that Marcus dabbled in soft drugs, but it wasn't really surprising that he had a bit of grass, hash that sort of thing. All students did. He was at university, that's what happened. That is what young people did at university. Got drunk, smoked draw, and studied at odd moments in between. As he drove down the street, he wondered if the flat he shared with a couple of other students had been raided or something. He supposed that they might have enough on them to cause a bit of trouble. But dealing? He couldn't believe it.

He pulled up outside the police station and turned off the lights, pausing a moment to gather his thoughts. Just as he was about to get out of the car, someone tapped on the window. He turned to see the front of a uniform and wound down the window.

'You can't park here. Double yellows.' The policeman bent down to look at Harry.

'I've just come to pick up my son. I won't be a tick.'

'You still can't park here.'

'Oh for Christ's sake. I'm in the job. My fucking son's just been nicked. Give me a break.'

'Look, pull round the back. There's a couple of spaces round there. But be quick.'

'Thanks.'

Harry found a space and jogged round to the front of the station. As he walked up the steps the door opened and Louise and Marcus appeared.

'What the bloody hell is going on?' Harry demanded. He could see the headlines now, son of detective sergeant charged with dealing drugs.

'Dad.' Marcus looked sheepish.

'It's all right he's been released on bail pending charges. Or something like that.' Louise looked tired and drawn.

'Oh, that's okay then.' He glared at them both. 'Look, I've parked the car round the back, let's go home, I don't want to do this on the street.'

They walked in crocodile fashion, Marcus at the rear, to the car. Harry didn't trust himself to speak again until they were in the flat. He threw his keys on to the table and turned on Marcus.

'Well?' He demanded.

'It's not what you think, dad, I just had a bit more on me than I should have done. I'm not dealing. I just sell to friends. The bastards busted me for no good reason.'

'How much?'

'How much what?'

'How much did you have on you?'

'Couple of grams of hash, bit of skunk, a few tabs.'

'Oh, well,' Harry threw his hands up in the air, 'nothing to get upset about.'

He looked at his son. His fair hair came from Tanya; in fact he seemed to have inherited none of the classic dark looks of his ancestry. He was slim, tall; god knows where that had come from. Tanya was petite and the men on his side of the family bordered on the stocky. For one awful moment he wondered if Marcus was really his son at all.

Louise perched on the arm of one of the small sofas. 'I think you'd better get it all out in the open Marcus, he'll find out sooner or later anyway.'

'Find out what?' Harry shouted.

Marcus cringed. 'I've been busted before.'

'You've what?' Harry's voice dropped to a soft growl, which was altogether more menacing.

'He's been busted before, he just told you, apparently they let him off with a caution. He wasn't carrying much.'

Harry shook his head. 'Yes, but they must have had some reason for picking you up, they must have suspected you were dealing?'

'It was a set-up. I didn't know the bloke was a copper.'

'I think the first rule of undercover work is that you don't wear your uniform on the job. Marcus, for Christ's sake, they must have been watching you for some time. Haven't you ever seen Cops on Sky, they do it all the time, and they have a fair idea of who the suspect is in the first place.'

'Sorry, dad.'

'It's you who might be sorry. The consequences are not good, you'll get kicked out of university, and that will be the least of your worries. I think you might even be facing a jail sentence.'

Marcus looked glum.

'God knows what your mother is going to say.'

'She knows already, I phoned her, but she was in the middle of one of her tarot sessions and couldn't come. That's why Louise phoned you.'

'Oh, fucking marvellous.'

'Sorry, I did ask her.'

'Marcus,' Harry reached over and touched his son's arm. 'I didn't mean you shouldn't have called me, I just would have thought under the circumstances…"

'Yeah.'

Louise stood up. "I'll make some coffee, perhaps we should speak to a lawyer."

"Just one more question Marcus, then I'll shut up. Where did you get the dope?"

Marcus looked away. "Whay dad, what are you going to do if I tell you?"

"You don't need to know, and I promise that nobody will ever know that you, or me, was involved at all. Trust me, son."

"It was little bloke, foreign, might be a Cypriot, I dunno, but's he's covered in gold, drives a red Merc, he hangs around the clubs down the Cally."

Mungo!

Home to Mum

The North Sea was swept before a rolling wind that bit at Harry's ears, bringing tears to soft eyes as it roared fiercely and crashed onto the fragile shore. It was no more than just a dull mass until he looked closely at the water as it tossed across the surface to see yellow, brown, deep green, a whole mix of colours in the swirling water with a deep palette like oil on the surface.

Louise seemed beyond the hazy distance of his horizon. Beyond reach. Far out to sea he could see a jumble of water, small wavelets lapping together in a random pattern. Close to her he felt hidden forces swelling. Their romance had moved on, but where was it going? It had started like a new shape that rears up from the surface of the sea. In that fraction of time the water coalesces to build a wave, which grows larger as it journeys towards the land. Harry felt he had been carried along, was it unwittingly?

She had taken over his life. It was no longer his life that was certain but was that so bad? He was content with his new life. They were comfortable together. She laughed at his jokes, and he enjoyed her body. It was a good life. Like the wave she was an individual, with her own character. The wave had arched its back to build a huge roll of water that would crash down on the foreshore. Would she do the same? Was he no more than a convenient excuse for her to get away from Justin?

Justin. There was a problem. Suddenly he had realised he had a partner that he cared about, and he wanted her to be with him, all the time. Somehow Justin had discovered Harry's flat, then his name, then where he worked, and telephone numbers. He knew how to use the phone. And he did, too often for Harry's sensibility. There always seemed to be a new valid excuse why he should want to talk to Louise. The bills to be paid, the window-cleaner, who was the washing-machine repair man she had called last time, what was Aunt Ellie's address. They just went on and on. It was all too cosy, too middle-class. He'd have understood if the guy had arrived on the doorstep with baseball bat in his hand, not that Justin needed a weapon to frighten the living daylights out of Harry. His size was more than enough.

Harry watched as his chosen wave swept towards the shore. It was a wave that had more energy than any wave that had gone before. Welling up from the depths like a whale, a mound of immense power gathering speed as it rose higher, and higher still until its very crest began to break into white foam. He could see that from that moment the wave was doomed. What about Louise and Harry? He didn't know where it was going now.

That Justin was not going to let go, not that easily. Harry could have coped with threats of violence, with outbursts of anger. Passion was, in some respects, his business. Criminals were often passionate angry people. Justin was a lawyer. A cold calculating leech that would suck them both dry before he finally let go.

Life began and ended without time. The breaking flash of white along the wave rim now showed this was not to be a great wave. It was already a has-been. All force gone, lost in the sprays of foam, like rushing cream, spurting and rolling forward deliciously as it rode atop the monster. For a few precious moments there had been beauty, joy and potential. That was the moment to yell 'Yes' in a raucous bellow of joy.

Then it was over. In an instant the wave was gone, now no more than swell, lost like a fat bellied porpoise to the following wave. The awesome majesty once promised spent by the foaming crest that was both its crowning glory and its demise. Magnificence destroyed as the wave peaks just before its time, so losing munificence and respect.

Much had been promised. Harry had wanted it to work with Louise. She was a nice girl. Is that the right word to describe anyone, let alone Louise? She was nice. She was sweet, she was funny, she was great in bed, she laughed at his jokes, she didn't cause much fuss, she organised his life. He now had time to enjoy.

That wave could have become the standard against which all subsequent waves would be compared. The wave's uppermost edge was broken by spume only when it was to begin the last great rear at the shore. That was the moment when white should have crackled atop, just as it stood upright, poised like a matador waiting to thrust downwards with all its strength on to the gravels beneath. That was the supreme unleashing moment. Then we would have marvelled as it crashed upon the hapless sands, with a thunderous roar, shattering itself into myriad droplets of white gushing spray.

Then there would have been no need to talk of its aftermath, as the gravels rattled under the belly of the next wave. The memory of that wave would have lived on, until the next stood poised above the shore.

Harry stood quietly, watching the rolling waves as they tracked towards the shore. He wanted to wrap his arms around her warmth. He needed to know they would come together again, and again. To understand that waves are just the surface of desire.

Slowly he walked back to his parent's house, in reflective mood. He enjoyed his work, but it was a sordid business. It hardened folk. All the pain and stress of other people's lives falling in your lap all the time. Perhaps it was time to move on. Do something different. He'd sort out this damned drug dealer, Mungo, and then think it out again. He was determined to sort out Mungo first. Nobody messed with his son, and got away with it. Besides Mungo had to be in the frame for the Winston business. That should be a murder investigation, and we need to talk to Mungo. Why was his car found in York? At a racecourse? He'd get the CCTV cameras sorted out once he got back. They might show something.

As for Louise he still wasn't sure it was going to work. What did he have to offer such a woman? Really? She was a vivacious intelligent pretty woman. OK, she was having it a bit tough right now. She'd made a few mistakes, but didn't we all? They couldn't last. He was just a stop-gap until something better came along. She was playing a game at present. All this 'I want to be a novelist' bit would pass as soon as some young buck happened by, loaded with more than just money and promised her a good time. She'd be off then.

Harry would then face the same scenes as before. The 'I'm working late tonight darling. Don't wait up and no, I'll grab at sandwich here.' Leaving the feeling that grips your stomach as you put down the phone. Being in the helpless inevitability of it all. He'd gone back home one afternoon when married to Tanya. She'd come running down the stairs, pulling on clothes, guilt written all over her face. He'd pushed her aside and raced upstairs, only to stand outside the toilet door listening to the frantic scramble of the man locked on the other side of the door. He'd stood outside as a wave of anger swept through his body, only to be overtaken by a terrible tiredness. What was the point of attacking this bloke, whoever he was? He'd just taken advantage of an offer. This was Tanya's house. It had been Tanya that had invited the guy back to have sex in her marital bed. How mean was that? How could Harry fight against that? For a marriage to work it needed the cooperation of both people. Marriage included a statement that said; 'I will not jump into bed with other people'. Or if I do, I'll damn sure that the other half of this relationship will never ever stand a chance of finding out. Tanya had wanted their marriage to end. She'd just banged a few obvious nails into its coffin. Eventually even Harry had bowed to the inevitable, and walked away, but he hadn't really stopped loving her. So how did all that fit in with Louise?

"Hi Mum." Harry smiled at the small figure standing at the kitchen sink.

"Hello son. Did you enjoy your walk?"

"Yes, it's good to be back beside the sea again. I'd forgotten." He looked across the room at the frail lady, grey-haired and stooped, recalling the faded photographs of a beautiful young woman, arm in arm with her new husband, strolling along that very same seafront. It's all too short, you have to take the opportunities you're offered.

As if she sensed his thoughts his mother looked up from the pile of carrots she was preparing.

"Make the most of it son. Have a good rest while you are here. I don't know how you stand that London, horrible dirty stinking smelly place, full of foreigners. I don't know what your granddad would say if he saw it now. What was that great war all about hey?" She straightened up, turning to drop a handful of carrots into a saucepan of water.

"I know mum. Times change. We're into ethnic diversity now."

She glanced back over her shoulder, a grim smile as she said, "And what does that mean? A lot of people coming here to take our jobs, and then take our money back from where they came from. Is that what it's all about?"

"Probably mum. All I know is that we can't change it. Somebody probably saw it as a way to make a quick buck I expect, and so in they all came. Better make the most of it, as it's not going to change."

She snorted, "Would do if I had my way. I wonder why we fight wars? So many good young men lose their lives, and for what? So a load of wasters and thieves could come in and take over? Those two world wars destroyed this country. All the good men gone, for ever. Better if we took all the politicians out and made them fight each other, that would change everything. They'd all do a bit more talking before they sent foolish young men out to fight for them."

"Yes mum, what are you cooking?"

She laughed, a quick titter as she swept up the saucepan and placed it on the stove. "Yes, alright, I know, I'm just a silly old biddy moaning on. Thought we'd have a bit of roast beef for a change. Don't do a big roast much these days, your dad and me don't eat that much and meat's so expensive. And I know you like a bit of Yorkshire pudding. Bet you don't get much of that in London, now do you?"

"No, you're right, I can't say that I do. But I do eat well these days. Bit too well really. I'm too happy and contented." He leant forward, arms over the kitchen table, reaching for the bowl of dried fruit and nuts that were always there.

"So tell me more about your new young lady? I see you didn't think we were good enough to bring down to see us. Why's that? Are we not good enough for her?

"Aw mum, don't be silly. She's lovely, you'll like her, and I know she'll like you. It's just that she's writing a book and wanted some time to get on with it, without me fussing around her all the time."

"You take care my boy. You've spent too much of your life fretting over these young girls. Don't know why you can't make a proper life for yourself instead. Just think how much money you've wasted, let alone anything else. That Tanya took you for every penny and then dumped you when something better came along, and as for the next little dolly-dripping, what you saw in her I shall never know."

There was much bashing and clattering of pans, knives and forks and plates for several minutes as she fussed around the kitchen. What could he say? She was right. His mum always was right, it was just that he'd never really listened to her very much before. Tanya had used him, like an appendage, a trophy to be marched around town, introduced to ever more acquaintances and then dropped, much as a bored cat walks away from the dead mouse.

Was that the right analogy? Had he been OK while he was alive and kicking? Was it his fault that Tanya had lost interest? Had he become a dead mouse? He was rather boring. Middle-aged. His marriages had been little more than attempts to brighten up his life. Tanya was worldly-wise, she needed to be the life and soul of the party, and his next conquest had just been a reaction to that world. He'd thrown aside the veneer of social gleam for a Bohemian approach where money was replaced by meaningful phrases.

Neither had really held much attraction for him. He'd never wanted a Maseratti or even a smart Italian suit, never yearned for expensive holidays in exotic locations, or to be part of the perfect world where everyone was judged by their possessions. He'd quickly found that the alternative world was hardly much better. Dependency upon drugs, having to rely upon anything for support, was demeaning and outside of his experience.

He looked again at his mother. Elderly now, hands gnarled by arthritis, face lined with age, but she was what she was, and that was obvious to anyone who came into contact with her. When he'd been younger she had appeared shallow, overly concerned with keeping the house clean and tidy, ensuring his father's tie was straight, even that he'd combed his hair properly before being allowed out of the house. Over the years he came to appreciate the real meaning to his parents lives. They loved and cared about each other, they loved him. They had a small circle of good friends, many of whom went back decades. They were part of their local community, and found pleasures in the daily communications with postman, shopkeeper, neighbour. They joined in the local social scene, his father as member of the Lodge and at the allotment, his mother with weekly teas and shopping trips with friends, and the Women's Institute.

They know their place, and they are content to be there. Harry wondered where he was. Is what I've done with my life an improvement upon that lived by my parents? Am I really more worthwhile because I've been to college, smoked pot, been to bed with a dozen women, caught a few criminals?

THE END

Printed in the United Kingdom
by Lightning Source UK Ltd.
122949UK00001B/94-117/A